Dead in the Water

Chasewater Mysteries Book One

Andy Hollyhead

CONTENTS

PROLOGUE

April 2022

The night shift had been much like any other patrol: sat in the car, sipping a coffee from the local McDonald's, and trying not to go mad with boredom whilst listening to the chatter on the Airwave radio.

Jack Appleyard's colleague wasn't his regular oppo who had been off work sick with stress for months and was unlikely to return. So, Jack was working with Phil, a Special Constable. Effectively volunteers, they were usually only wheeled out for community events and crowd control at football matches. A perfect storm of recent cuts to the police budget, conflicts with holiday rotas, and the general bureaucratic screw up that appeared to permeate the culture of West Midlands police, particularly those working out of Brownhills police station, meant this sort of thing was becoming increasingly commonplace.

In contrast, Phil was as excited as it is possible to be - his first shift as a special and he was out on patrol. Okay the most demanding thing asked of him so far was to remember Jack's coffee order, but the girl in McDonald's had smiled at him and let him off paying for the scalding hot liquid, though not unfortunately for the blueberry muffin that Jack had also insisted upon. He'd heard that freebies were often given to regular officers, and he was pleased as punch that he had been mistaken for one.

'How long have you been a copper?' This was a standard opening line for any blue light staff and Phil thought he was on fairly safe ground in asking it of Jack.

'Too long,' was the terse reply. Jack really wasn't in the mood for idle chitchat. His sleep during the day had been particularly troubled. A light sleeper at the best of times, these Easter holidays his insomnia had been exacerbated by children playing outside during the day. Screams and shouts had punctuated involving both Russell Tovey and the England rugby squad.

Phil was taken aback a little by the monosyllabic reply, but he had been warned in advance by his Commanding Officer that PC Appleyard could be a 'funny bugger', as he had not so subtly put it.

The message that came through onto the police computer mounted on the dashboard sounded straightforward enough: 'Any available officers head to Linden Road, report of an intruder at the rear of number twenty-eight.'

'That's us', Jack said. 'Two hundred yards away, we don't even have to take the panda. Punch it in.' Phil winced at the arcane term but tapped the relevant code into the computer console to indicate that they had responded to the call.

The row of Victorian terraced houses had an access alley to the rear, wide enough to allow a car to be driven down. Most of the homes had converted some or all of their backyards into parking with a prefab concrete garage or hardstanding area, leaving just a narrow back gate for access to what remained of the garden. In this area of the Black Country the front door continued to be only used by many families for funerals and weddings, the back door into the kitchen was the main entrance to the house.

One back gate was open, and at two in the morning the sound of it swinging on its rusty hinges seemed to be amplified in the still spring air. Both Jack and Phil's footsteps, and Phil's slightly laboured breath could be heard from a way off. They found themselves consciously trying to draw their breath quietly as they approached the rear of number twenty-eight. Jack rolled his eyes at Phil's wheezing breath, could they have arrived any more noisily he thought to himself.

Jack motioned to Phil to hold back, both hands palm down to attempt to indicate stealth. Though whether Phil was pumped full of adrenaline or just didn't see the gesture in the poorly lit passage, Jack never knew, and berated himself for months afterwards, wishing he had somehow physically restrained his colleague.

With a loud shout of, 'Police! Don't move!' Phil ran headlong into the backyard, pushing the gate with his left hand, baton in the other.

The Special Constable never knew what hit him as the teenage yob who was hiding directly behind the gate swung the head of a gardening shovel directly at the constable's face, flooring him and rendering him unconscious immediately.

The thug continued to run through the gate and straight into the arms of Jack Appleyard. It was over in a matter of seconds.

If the police car had been parked closer, the Investigating Officer would later claim, the eighteen-year-old looking for garden equipment he could sell at the local car boot to fund his weed habit could have been bundled into the back of it. Therefore help for the stricken officer would then have come more quickly. But even though Jack had called for assistance as soon as possible, Phil had suffered a catastrophic brain injury, not so much from the impact of the shovel, but his impact on the ground and the hard standing.

Both his Commanding Officer and the Investigating Officer weren't the only ones asking those questions. Rehabilitation for Phil would be long and slow. The prognosis was that he would most likely be confined to a wheelchair for the rest of his life.

In some ways the suspension, delivered in person by his Commanding Officer another few sleepless days later, had come as something of a relief. His working life was in the hands of someone else now. All the right channels were being covered; his Police Federation representative had already been in contact to ensure that Jack's side of the story was consistent and correct, which it always would be. Jack had never lied to the veteran silver-haired officer, there was no need to. Phil was not a reliable witness, the injury had wiped his memory from the moment he left the McDonald's clutching the two coffees, though he could precisely remember the order.

Call it 'Special Leave' or 'Gardening Leave', whatever euphemism was used the outcome was the same. Jack had been suspended on full pay, and four months later there was no clear end in sight. His life had taken on a new rhythm, but not as yet a new meaning.

CHAPTER ONE

August 2022

The forecast had said it would be another hot day. The heatwave that had lasted for much of the previous month showed no signs of breaking. Even now, just after eleven in the morning, there was a shimmering haze over the water, and the crowds would appreciate it being another scorcher.

Chasewater at the weekend possessed a completely different atmosphere to the much quieter weekdays. During the week the man-made reservoir - built in the eighteenth century to ensure that the canals of Birmingham had sufficient water for the locks and weirs, was relatively peaceful. Nothing more than polite nods and the odd greeting between its various users disturbed the peace. Dog walkers, bird spotters and joggers ruled the land, and on the water only the occasional windsurfer could be seen from the shore. At weekends however, children on bikes and family groups overwhelmed the land, whilst on the water the windsurfers were joined by wakeboarders pulled by an electric tow cable up at the top pier near the two popular cafés, and water skiers towed by powerful speed boats made the water a vibrant place, buzzing with activity. There was always something to watch, and the cafés, ice cream stands, and crazy golf concession did a booming trade, at least during the long summer days.

This Sunday was something different, though. Not seen in Staffordshire for many years, the Power Boat Grand Prix had returned to Chasewater. Small, noisy craft piloted (usually) by young men were painted in vivid hues. Their sponsorship by various energy drink manufacturers created bright-coloured ribbons as they raced around a mile-long circuit in the middle of the reservoir in order to avoid shoreline erosion, weaving between the blue and orange marker buoys that delineated the route. The noise was incredible, even from a distance, and the carparks and overflow grass fields were full to bursting as families came to see the races. The wildlife which regarded Chasewater as their home were much less happy: the swans, geese and ducks preferred to shelter near the shoreline or in the unfortunately named Norton Bog, a quiet and smaller overflow pond, but those that forgot were still regularly buffeted by the wake from the boats as they passed, and bobbed indignantly on the water, their cries unheard over the roar of the engines.

The tannoy was audible only from a short distance away before fading out to a distant drone across the water. Those directly involved in the racing knew the rough schedule though. They frequently checked in with the marshals, who reassured them that their particular race time hadn't drifted too much from the planned timetable. The marquees and gazebos of the individual teams were as bright and gaudy as the boats, and camera drones whizzed over the water, controlled remotely through complex control pads manoeuvred by serious-looking men wearing peaked caps and Polaroid-filtered sunglasses.

All the picnic benches littering the water's edge had been taken by large family groups and were defended, fortress-like, from any unsuspecting clans silly enough to try and invade their space. Despite being against the rules, portable barbecues had also been lit across the waterfront and the smell of roasted meat permeated the air. Fluorescent windbreakers acted as psychological and physical barriers for others, shielding them from the gaze of passers-by. Everywhere the murmur of voices could be heard, mingling with children's screams at some imagined slight, and the barking of various dogs, who must have been wondering at what had happened to their normally quiet and peaceful paradise.

Mingling amongst the crowd were a small cadre of serious-looking men, who despite the heat, favoured black jeans and the heavy sleeveless body warmers replete with pockets full of unknown technical equipment. This invariably meant they had red faces, and a sheen that wasn't entirely due to poorly applied sunscreen. A passing observer may have thought they were security guards, ever-present at any public event, but the lack of high-visibility vests and walkie-talkies would have dissuaded that thought. Slung over their shoulders were folded-up tripods, and expensive cameras with unfeasibly large, phallic lenses hanging from them. Some of these were semi-professional photographers, who followed the powerboats across Britain and even further afield. They sold their photos to websites, magazines and sometimes even the teams themselves, for publicity or promotional shots. Other 'men in black' were just enthusiastic amateurs, taking photos for the simple pleasure of creating a good picture, posting online to get 'likes' or retweets and more followers. One of these was Martin Barr.

Martin had not really enjoyed school. Whilst there were people he would call schoolmates, he never saw them beyond the school gates. No Duke of Edinburgh Awards or sports clubs filled his time after school. Instead, it was home, onto his Playstation and the latest game.

His favourite subject whilst there was Geography, and the memories of a two-day field trip in his final year at school still remained with him five years after. Glan-llyn in the heart of Wales was an excellent location to study glacial erosion, terminal moraines, and the other physical geographical features much-loved by year eleven students. The views from the bunk house windows each morning were amazing. Always a light sleeper, the thin curtains had offered little protection from the early morning dawn. The sun appeared to hit and shimmer off Llyn Tegid, better known to people as Lake Bala, before it fully illuminated the sky. The only disturbance was the heavy breathing and snores of the three other classmates, and the incessant birdsong as the dawn chorus started.

One evening, completely against the many safety briefings they had received, one of the lads in the group had found that the rusting shipping container that stored the canoes was unlocked - for who would steal anything from such a remote basecamp? The teachers, in a moment of madness, decided that it would be a good idea for a dozen inexperienced students to head out onto the lake unescorted, it's possible that they had a wine box of their own to finish off and they hadn't made the best judgment call of their careers. Luckily the life jackets were also within the container, otherwise the frequent capsizing that inevitably followed could have been disastrous. Despite the summer heat, the water was still icy cold. Martin was splashed many times by the paddles of others, sometimes accidently, sometimes with more malicious intent to remind him that he was still very much an outsider.

It was that evening that Martin remembered now, as he stood on the pier that jutted out into Chasewater, power boats creating a spray as they surged past, their bow waves disturbing the wildlife still trying to take shelter in the shallower water by the shore. Whilst the feeling of heat and cold were similar to that experienced ten years ago, there were two differences: the huge crowds that had turned out to watch, and the noise that the boats made as they passed, a low drone with a bass that made the teeth vibrate at a particular frequency, especially after hours of observation trying to get the perfect shot.

He had been positioned on the outcrop for most of the day, only reluctantly yielding his place to other spectators to relieve himself, at the toilet block or when that became more and more disgusting as the day went on, a short stroll to the trees that surrounded the reservoir. When he returned inevitably his spot had been taken, but the usurpers eventually wandered off between races, Martin's steely gaze and passive-aggressive body language quickly restoring the status quo. Though slight of frame, his height could intimidate all but the tallest of people, something that he had found useful in his job until only recently.

The amateur photographer filled two

memory cards with photos and video shots of the races, panning the camera from right to left as the power boats zoomed past, taking many shots per second. Despite the stifling heat, he still wore his many-pocketed utility vest. The casual observer would think that he was one of the professional photographers. It would take him hours to sort through the thousands of shots taken in his bedroom back home, but he had the time.

He looked at his watch and decided that he would indeed stay on for another half hour for the last race at four o'clock. The crowds had thinned out significantly. Indeed, he was metaphorically king of the castle, and his views were now unobstructed. His Digital SLR camera was an impressive-looking piece of kit, the most expensive thing he owned in fact, and he fired off some random shots, zooming in on the causeway of the dam on the eastern side of the reservoir.

Couples and families were slowly heading back towards the main car park. There was the smell of a barbecue further back, but he couldn't really see any of the rangers complaining on such a perfect day. Martin could see a large, animated group of maybe eight or ten people, a broad range of ages from toddler to grandparents. They had four dogs with them, two small ones of indeterminate breed, and two French Bulldogs, darting through the legs of the group like a moving slalom course, laughing at the antics of their four-legged friends.

Martin started walking back home. It wasn't far at all by foot, but by car it was a circuitous journey round the lake and onto the ring road taking at least two miles. The rucksack of equipment was heavy on his back. He would be glad to get home, polish his lenses and put the battery packs on charge ready for his next expedition. He could feel his back becoming moist with sweat from the heat, and pledged he would get some cooler, safari-style clothing if he was going to do more photography in this heat. He was looking forward to making himself some tea, eating it in his room away from his mum and stepdad, and then an early night to start looking through the pictures tomorrow.

He skirted the edge of the lake, despite there being quicker routes, camera hung around his neck, looking for that final shot. Who knows? He may even catch something other than wildlife. He remembered the picture he'd taken earlier in the day of some lads skinny dipping, egging each other on. Maybe Fish would get a thrill out of the pics. They were about his age.

He was aware of footsteps behind him, but this wasn't unusual. The countryside surrounding the reservoir was emptying quickly now the racing had finished. He carried on, increased his pace. Something didn't feel right. He quickened, and with his spare hand grabbed the keys in his pocket, pushing the point of his house key between his clenched fingers, forming an improvised knuckle-duster. No one was going to try and take his camera equipment from him.

Chasewater Railway had been particularly busy on Sunday because of the powerboat racing on the water. Run by volunteers for over fifty years, the line ran in a long arc across half of the circumference of the reservoir, taking a gentle forty-five minutes to amble the three miles to the end of the line, where they swapped the engine then returned back the way it had come.

Due to the risk of fire from sparks coming from the chimney igniting the dry scrubland on the surrounding heath, the three ancient commuter carriages hadn't been steam hauled, but pulled by a heritage diesel on the hourly service. A non-timetabled, special last train had been put on later than usual at six o'clock, to pick up stragglers across the two stations and the other request stops and get them back to the main carparks at either end. The volunteer drivers didn't mind, and the guards on the train were always happy to ride the short distance one more time at the end of the day.

The heat had started to cool, and the passengers were all listless as they gently trundled back to the main depot for one last time. At least the incessant drone of the powerboats had now ceased, and the steady sound of the carriages on the tracks had sent many of the passengers into a torpor.

Around half-way back there was a narrow causeway that the line crossed, separating two parts of the reservoir. Jeffrey's Swag was a smaller fishing lake and haven for the rarer wading wild birds, the main reservoir being dominated by wildlife that was happy in the deeper water.

As always there were two drivers in the Class 08 shunter, a lumbering diesel engine with poor forward visibility and a maximum speed of twenty-five miles per hour, a speed never attempted or achieved on the Chasewater Line. The senior driver, Tom, a volunteer for over twenty years, was looking out of the right-side of the engine through the small porthole window and down onto the track as the line crossed the causeway. They always slowed down below walking pace and blew the horn just in case there were any idiots walking on the sleepers trying to take a short cut.

George was one of the younger engine drivers. This was his first season at the railway, having already decided he was unlikely to volunteer next year. He'd be off to university anyhow, and it would be difficult to fit in time at Chasewater along with the part-time job, which he had been told in no uncertain terms by his father that he would have to get.

With Tom's foot on the dead-man's pedal and the other on the speed control, there was little left for George to do. He was staring out of the left-hand window, half looking forward but mostly looking down into the water, 'daydreaming' as he would reluctantly admit to the police later.

As the train approached the end of the causeway, he thought he saw a bundle of sodden clothing that had caught itself under the bridge. As it drew his eye however, something wasn't quite right. As they slowly trundled over the bridge, he could make out firstly a red bloom in the water, and then with a shout recognised that the mass of blood, clothing and flesh was shaped like human body.

With a shout of, 'Stop!' he grabbed the braking wheel. Tom took his foot of the dead-man's pedal and the engine came to a shuddering halt.

'What's up, George?' Tom could see that his co-driver had turned pale, despite the sweat and inevitable grime on his face from working the engine.

'Jesus, there's something in the water!'

'Let's have a look then, clear out of the way.' George shuffled round to the other side of the cramped cab, making way for Tom. He looked back over the causeway, as many others on the train pushed the windows down too to look out and see what had caused the emergency stop. In the distance the wail of a child could be heard, almost like an air-raid siren starting up.

The subsequent screams and shouts of passengers in the first carriage confirmed George's worst fears. Tom, ever pragmatic, put a reassuring arm on Tom's shoulder, as he cowered in the corner.

'Move the train on lad, the passengers don't need to see any more of this. I'll call the police.'

CHAPTER TWO

Jack Appleyard seemed to be sleeping in later these days. Usually an early riser, both the summer heatwave and his chronic insomnia had recently got the better of him. Why bother getting up at seven when he might be able to catch a few extra hours of sleep missed the previous night? He allowed his clock radio to continue to quietly murmur to itself and drifted off again.

He stirred as Radio WM, the local BBC radio station started the mid-morning show, the thick Brummie accent cutting through his half-formed dreams. Jack couldn't stand the adverts of the commercial radio stations, though the constant plugging of other BBC stations and the newly launched BBC Sounds application was also getting on his nerves. Lots of things got on his nerves recently, however. Reluctantly, he opened his eyes, scratched himself down below and started his day. The usual routine of shave, shower and shovelling cereal down his throat was completed almost totally on automatic pilot. It was the ten o'clock news that registered with Jack that something was different. He must have dozed through the previous news bulletins, and it was only the last story that finally cut through his early morning fug.

'A person was tragically killed yesterday during a powerboat competition in Chasewater on the West Midlands and Staffordshire border. The person, who is yet to be identified, appears to have been caught in the propeller blades of a number of craft as they raced around the mile-long course. Police are asking for anyone with any information to contact the police on 101.'

Jack grimaced at the mention of propellor blades. He knew what that meant: dismemberment or decapitation of the body was inevitable. Identifying the poor lad was not going to be easy. If he had been swimming (or skinny dipping he thought to himself) to cool off in the intense August heat, people rarely went swimming with their driving license with them. And if a DNA profile wasn't already in the database, it would be a matter of waiting until missing person reports were filed, or long-standing files were sifted through for significant scars. Even dental records may not be of much use, depending on the state of the body. Jack gulped. He was close to losing his recently eaten breakfast just thinking about it.

Jack reviewed the news report in his mind. They had said 'person's body', he had just assumed that it was a man. Was the corpse so badly mangled they couldn't even tell the gender of the victim yet?

He opened the browser on his phone. The BBC news site had little to add to the report - indeed, it was almost verbatim the report that the radio bulletin had issued. A wider Google search revealed nothing, they sometimes took a while to catch up with events. Even the local newspapers weren't running the story yet. It must have broken very late the night before, on Sunday evening when most news editors and reporters had cleared off early to enjoy the good weather. Pimm's and lemonade under the gazebo, Jack imagined.

Social media wasn't much better. The official West Midlands Police account repeated the plea for help and expressed their condolences to the family, assuming the person had any. Searching for key words and hashtags relating to the area - Chasewater, Burntwood, Brownhills - yielded nothing more than the usual local commentators blaming the local councils, the police, or immigrants for what appeared to have been a tragic accident.

A few quick texts to his colleagues - he still thought of them as such even though his suspension was now entering its fourth month - yielded no results, either. Some simply ignored the message, though he could see that they had been read. Others replied with short messages saying that they knew nothing about the case, which was a clear lie. This was the biggest thing to happen in the area for months, if not years, and all uniformed police from Brownhills Police Station, his old headquarters, would be involved. Jack was sure of that.

Only his old friend, Tracey Bullock, replied in anything like a friendly tone, suggesting a coffee after her shift later that day. Jack readily agreed and started rummaging through his wardrobe for something reasonable to wear. The temptation to head up to the reservoir now, to be at the scene of whatever had happened, was great, but for now he was going to have to be a little patient. He slipped into blue cargo shorts and a clean white T-shirt with the pride logo subtly embroidered on the sleeve. Blue canvas deck shoes would complete the look for him to head out.

He tried to divert his energies into something else and made a half-hearted attempt to tidy his apartment. He had bought it shortly after completing his probation period nearly nine years ago, and at first the mortgage payments had been crippling. However now, they were much more affordable than what many of his colleagues were paying for rent, and he had no intention of moving, even when the noise of children playing outside frequently drove him to distraction. Three bedrooms just for him was an indulgence, he knew, but one was an office where he (used to) study for his sergeants' examinations. The second bedroom, for years he had rented out to friends and friends of friends. It was now restored to the status of being a guest bedroom, though most of his overnight guests were not interested in staying in a separate bed, at least until Jack started snoring.

Checking the time on his phone, he realised he was going to have to get a move on if he was going to be on time for his late lunch 'date'. He checked himself in the mirror. It was a good job the 'just got out of bed' look suited his black hair, with just a touch of product to keep the short quiff in check. A quick smile to himself to try and restore some confidence before closing the apartment door and Jack ran down the two flights of stairs to his car.

The BJ Diner had been perched on the main road between Cannock and Lichfield for many years. Part of a small chain, its precarious existence was owed partly to the novelty factor of being a retro fifties-style American restaurant, but mostly to passing trade, the majority of whom didn't know better and were unlikely to visit again.

With surly staff and indifferent service, the clientele on a Monday afternoon was a strange mix of salespeople needing a caffeine fix before hitting the road, and local mums with their toddlers, driven to distraction during the long summer holidays and trying to find some way of keeping them entertained.

Jack and Tracey took one of the booths tucked away to the rear of the diner and placed their orders quickly, barely glancing at the menu. The attraction of the locality for them both was the unlimited free refills of coffee and, more importantly for this meeting, the low chance of any superior officers walking in. The garish decor of bright red leatherette, and shiny chrome and stainless steel seemed to glare even more brightly in the unfiltered August sun, but the air conditioning was pumping out freezing air, and Jack was wishing that he had slipped a hoodie on as well.

'It's good to see you. It's been too long,' Tracey said. A few years older than Jack, her dark brown hair was cut in a sensible bob, which seemed to phase in and out of fashion. She seemed twitchy, which Jack didn't believe was solely due to the coffee.

'I've been busy. Well, I haven't, but...' Jack sighed and stirred the grey coffee, adding too much sugar as always.

'So why did you get in touch? You know I'm breaking all sorts of rules - well, guidelines - by even talking to you.'

'I know, I know, and I do appreciate it, I really do. I just want to know more about what's happened up at Chasewater. Come on Tracey, you know something, don't you?'

'What makes you think I know anything? As far as I know it's a tragic accident. The poor lad...'

'We know he was male, then?' Jack

interrupted.

'Yeah, we've been able to confirm that, but there's not much else to help with identification. Looks like one of the racing speedboats, you know there was some competition going on?' Jack nodded, he'd seem something on his Twitter feed a few days back but hadn't paid it much attention, it wasn't his sort of thing. 'Well, seems that one of the speed freaks must've hit him and knocked him out, and he drifted into the path of the other boards.' Tracey looked down at her rapidly congealing eggs. She had suddenly lost her appetite. The all-day breakfast had been a mistake at two o'clock in the afternoon.

Jack locked eyes with Tracey. 'Do you really believe that, though?'

Tracey paused before answering. 'It doesn't matter what I believe, Jack. I'm a PCSO, they're not going to share the results of any findings with me, are they?'

'I don't know. Community liaison and all that, they may be reaching out to you to... I don't know, reassure people, maybe?'

'I've got enough on my plate looking after neighbourhood disputes and bloody dogs barking. You know what my last call was before my shift ended? A complaint about a toddler scratching the side of someone's car.'

Jack smiled. This rant of Tracey's, and variations on the same theme, was all too familiar. Indeed, he had his own similar story to tell anyone who thought that the life of a copper must be glamorous.

'OK, OK, I understand. But if there's nothing official, there must be some rumours, something from the post-mortem. Come on, I'm not going to hold you to it in court, am I?'

'I did hear something. One of the new detective sergeants was mouthing off in the canteen. I don't think you know him, he arrived, after... you know.' Tracey looked sheepish, and Jack shifted his gaze onto the only reasonably attractive waiter in the diner. Realising he was staring too hard he brought himself back to the conversation.

'What was that, then?'

'It seems there was no water in the lungs - well, the left lung anyhow, the right one was too squished to be sure.'

'So that means he was dead before he was in the water?'

'Seems like that, but as you heard the body was pretty messed up. We don't know if there was a natural cause before he was, you know, food processed.' She made a twisting motion with both hands and pulled a face.

'That's a bit graphic.' Jack mimicked her face. Anyone looking in through the window of the American diner at the time might have wondered if they were entering a gurning competition.

'Sorry, forgot you were always a lightweight when it comes to this sort of thing.'

'One last question - well, a favour really.'

'I'm not going to do anything that will get me into more trouble, talking to you. It's bad enough that we're meeting now.'

'Just let me know if you hear anything else about the case. Anything that might not make it onto Facebook or Twitter, know what I mean?'

'So, you want me to break more rules, beyond talking to a suspended police officer? Why not, it's not like I have anything better to do in my time off.'

'I know, and I really do appreciate it.' A pause, then, 'How's... you know, whats his name?'

'You mean Gavin, my boyfriend these last four years?'

'Yeah, yeah, sorry.'

In response, Tracey held up her left hand, showing off her new engagement ring. 'He proposed!'

Jack looked nonplussed before he quickly composed himself and shifted to a broad smile that to him felt totally artificial and forced, but Tracey was too self-absorbed at that moment to notice.

'Last month. We've yet to sort out a day.'

'Congratulations. Seriously, Gavin is a lucky man'.

Jack had never got round to sharing with anyone, especially Tracey, that one drunken night in Birmingham a year or so previously he and Gavin had shared a not-to-brief fumble in the back of Snobs nightclub when Tracey had disappeared to the loo. Ah well, he thought, another one lost. He'd better delete Gavin's number from his phone, along with the pictures they had exchanged shortly afterwards on WhatsApp.

'Are you listening to me Jack?'

'Hmm? Sorry, I was miles away.'

'Anyone nice? Anyhow, as I was saying, Gavin has his best man sorted, but you'll go to his stag do, won't you? Keep him on the straight and narrow.'

Jack gulped. 'I don't know, I don't really know him that well, do I? Stag nights aren't really my scene, all a bit too macho.'

'Nonsense, you'll be a good influence on the rest of the group, and I'll be happier knowing you're there. They're hardly going to go to a strip club with you in the group, are they?'

After leaving the diner, Jack hugged Tracey in the car park, and they went their separate ways. Tempting though the idea of a disco nap would have been to try and catch up on lost sleep. He decided instead to try his luck and see if he could get onto Chasewater. The drive was less than five minutes, and his red MINI Cooper raced past the plodding articulated trucks struggling up the gradient of the A5 to get onto the M6 Toll Road. He wondered how he had got to this point - not the suspension, he had gone over that so many times that it was almost as if he'd worn the record out and was in danger of suffering Post Traumatic

Stress Disorder. No, why did he think he could make a good copper in the first place?

Jack had managed to have an unconventional police career even before it had started. It wasn't *specifically* described as affirmative action, well not directly anyhow. But the fact that he was attracted to men and hadn't hidden the fact throughout any part of the application process may have helped him through some of the trickier parts of the process. Equality and Diversity had been the latest buzzwords.

The initial interviews were fine, the physical tests he aced without hardly breaking a sweat, but it was the psychological tests that were a cause of concern for his superiors, even at that time. 'Borderline personality disorder' was a term one recruitment sergeant had confided to the rest of the team, though he didn't actually write this down. The final interviewer was slightly more circumspect in the language he used.

'We were a little concerned about some of the test results. They seem to indicate that you may not be a team player?'

'I'm not sure what you mean by that?' Even ten years ago, Jack's habit of answering a question with a question was infuriating even for those who knew him well. For those that didn't, it could seem overly aggressive.

'Well, let's assume that you are patrolling as a pair and your colleague is attacked. The perpetrator runs away. What would you do?'

Jack had studied too many books on body language to be caught out in an interview with the basic errors, so he concentrated on showing an open and relaxed posture. Whilst he had no strong feelings either for or against the interviewer, he was also sure that he wasn't going to be intimidated by her, even if this was the final hurdle to be crossed before he realised his ambition of becoming a police officer. In years to come his posture would have been called 'manspreading': legs apart and arms reaching back to scratch his head. He took his time before replying.

'I would of course ensure my hypothetical partner was not going to be in any more danger, but my priority would be to get the rotten scrote that had done that to my partner, and so would probably give chase.'

'And if your partner became unconscious?'

Jack's fists clenched slightly, had he screwed up his entire application by being too honest?

'I did say that if he was not going to be in any more danger, I would give chase. Of course, if he wasn't breathing, he, or she of course, would have to be my first priority.' He had a feeling that his interviewer had gone off the fixed interview questions, and she was now struggling to regain control. She looked down at her notes, flustered. Jack smiled and realised that he was that final step closer to joining the force.

'Do you have any questions for me, Mr Appleyard.'

'No, I look forward to hearing from you soon.'

The sun was still blazing hot, despite it being mid-afternoon, as he turned into Chasewater, through the gates and the electronic sleeping policeman that attempted to prevent late night vehicles cruising. And other sorts of cruising, Jack mused. Stepping out of the car, the heatwave temperature hit him again. His canvas deck shoes offered little protection from the radiant heat of car park Tarmac.

He walked past the sculpture that marked the entrance to the country park, a strange concrete knot reminiscent of a cheap Henry Moore. He was amazed that it hadn't yet been vandalised. He remembered that it had been commissioned for a nearby primary school in the sixties. Then the artist had become very aggrieved that the pupils wanted to climb all over it, so placing it in the middle of the small traffic island as a sentinel to the country park seemed like a good idea to preserve its integrity, though most people cared less about its artistic meaning, long lost in the mists of time. Jack liked it though, as he did the whole of Chasewater, and had spent many happy hours here.

Stopping off at the café first for a secret weapon, he started the walk round to the causeway. It was a twenty-five minute stroll from where he'd parked. He had planned to see how far he could get, expecting to be turned away before long, but was surprised he could get close to Jeffrey's Swag. He anticipated encountering the blue Police tape well before now. Reduced staffing due to the recent police cuts had made an even bigger impact than maybe he expected, and Chasewater would be a very large area to cordon off.

He looked out to the reservoir. As expected, the only thing moving on the water was a single white motor launch with Police markings and an unnecessary blue flashing light. It was slowly crossing the full length of the water, backwards and forwards. They must have launched it from either the sailing club ramp on other side of the water, or motor sports compound further ahead, probably towed by a massive Range Rover. Two uniformed officers could just be discerned on the craft, one to port and one to starboard staring into the water, one holding what looked like fishing nets, the other a complex camera. Jack couldn't decide whether they had the best or worst job in this weather.

The trains weren't running of course, Tom and George's service the day before when the body have been discovered would be the last one until at least the following weekend. Jack had already checked that on the website. They would lose some income - the school holiday period and the glorious weather would have meant passenger numbers were on the up this week. But no doubt the police had been insistent that no trains run, and the trustees of the charity would have to understand.

Jack continued walking the footpath parallel to the line. About a hundred yards from the causeway there was an attempt at least to divert people. Blue police tape was strung between two convenient Hawthorn bushes on the path. 'Do Not Cross' the tape said, so he didn't. He simply stepped around the bush.

The second line was fifty metres further on, and this at least was being manned. He knew the uniformed PC Alan Ball well, he had been recruited around the same time as him, and his career had also continued the same dynamically flat trajectory that Jack's had, though for different reasons. Whilst Jack has always annoyed his commanding officers with his arrogance, Alan was the opposite. Obsequious to the chain of command, originality of thought was not one of his strong points. But he and Jack had got on OK, and at a small police station such as Brownhills that was probably a good job.

'Alan, how's things?'

'Jack! I didn't recognise you out of your uniform.' Well, it was a variation on a greeting, Jack supposed.

'I've brought you a drink. Coke or Fanta?' He reached into his messenger bag and proffered the still ice-cold bottles purchased from the café. As far as bribes went it wasn't the best, but it was all he had to work with.

Alan took the bottle of Fanta and opened it carefully. 'Thanks, really appreciated.' Jack noticed that the officer wasn't wearing his regulation black shirt, but the older style white shirt. Still smart but most definitely not regulation. The constable was still sweating profusely though despite the cooler shirt.

'When did you get on?'

'I started at two.' Glancing at his watch, he let out an audible groan. 'Jesus, is it only four?'

'Fraid so, mate. So have CID found anything yet?'

'It's not so much a body as a joint of meat, apparently. They think it was hit by at least three different boats, must have been like whack-a-mole. All the limbs are mauled, but he was wearing a gilet, like this.' Alan pointed to his own black utility waistcoat, replete with pockets filled with the accoutrements of the modern police officer, and of course his personal mobile phone. 'It offered the abdomen some protection, but not enough.'

'That sounds really… grizzly.'

'It is, but at least we've got something to go on for identification now.'

'Didn't they find his wallet?'

'No. That's what made us suspect that something's not quite right. If it had been a pissed bloke falling into the water then he'd have his phone, wallet, and car keys in the gilet, wouldn't he? All the pockets had been emptied.'

Jack was surprised how forthcoming Alan was being. Boredom and a friendly face maybe can do that, or maybe a touch of heat stroke. Jack wondered how much further he could push it.

'So, what do we have to identify the body? I mean victim?'

'Well, he did have a tattoo on his arse'.

'So? Lots of blokes I've seen have tattoos on backsides. You'd be surprised.'

Alan shuffled around uncomfortably. Even with all the equality and diversity training that the modern copper has to undergo, Alan had never been happy about Jack's wide open sexuality. Alan had married his childhood sweetheart at eighteen, had two children, a boy and a girl, quickly followed by the snip, and as far as he was concerned what he or anyone did in the bedroom was their own business.

'I'm sure you do, Jack, but this one is unique. Do you know anyone who has a TARDIS tattooed on his left arse cheek?'

Despite the heat, Jack felt icy cold as Alan continued to chat away about the unfairness of the situation that he felt himself in as the sole officer on duty on that approach to the crime scene. As soon as he could, he made his excuses and left. The chances of him being able to see a SOCO was minimal he knew, and anyhow it sounded like they were in the final stages of clearing things up. Walking back to the car, he stopped at one of the picnic benches dotted under the trees, grateful for the shade and also the opportunity to let him look at his phone more clearly out of the glare of the afternoon sun, which was shimmering off the water.

There was no sound other than the bird song, and the roar of the motorway which had cut through the area nearly twenty years earlier much to the local protester's dismay. No human voices however, it's amazing how a little bit of blue tape strung across a couple of bushed had the authority to stop people in their tracks.

He fired up Grindr on his iPhone, the gay hook-up app which he occasionally - who was he kidding? Quite frequently used to chat to and chat up guys. In reality, he rarely met up with anyone, and recently his own mojo had become non-existent as the uncertainty about his job continued to dominate his thoughts.

He scrolled through his recent chats (okay, maybe he was definitely more than occasional user of the app) and there he was. Marty McFly, clearly an alias. It showed he had last been active five days previously, so Marty was an occasional user, too. It had been a couple of months since they'd last exchanged greetings, and photos. All part of the game nowadays. He grimaced at the torso shot that he had sent to Marty, cropped at the head and with the hint of a treasure trail. He thought it was good practice, whilst there was a chance of still being a serving police officer, not to have half-naked pictures showing his face - or worse - circulating too wildly on social media.

He scrolled down. The usual platitudes of 'nice bod' and 'show more' and the usual string of emoticons. And then there it was: the photo that he remembered receiving.

The image of the blue time travelling machine, better known as a TARDIS, was conventional in appearance, without flourishes, around two inches tall. It looked strangely flat, which considering where it had been inked was a skill in itself. Jack's first horrible suspicions when he was talking to Alan was right. The body that had been found in Chasewater was that of 'Marty McFly', and worse, was 'known' to suspended PC Jack Appleyard.

Putting his phone away, he stared out at the water, wondering what to do next. Jack had the same feeling that he had when he scored an own goal for his school football team, a feeling which had been amplified tenfold that night four months previously when he realised Phil had been so seriously injured. It was a nauseating combination of guilt, shame, embarrassment, and panic - all combining in the pit of his stomach.

Even though he knew that messages would be stored on a central server somewhere, he deleted his message history from the app, and indeed went further and deleted the app itself.

He knew he hadn't eradicated the data, but just knowing that it was off his phone helped calm him just a little.

Still nervous, still edgy, he continued to walk back to his car. He knew the name of the victim, at least his alias, and he was sure it would be the work of moments for the digital forensics team to identify his real name from his screen name through the company's server. But what could he do with this information?

By the time he returned to his car he had got no further in his deliberations. He was so distracted on the way home that he nearly crashed twice. Only when he pulled safely into his allocated parking space, got inside, vomited in the toilet with the sheer shock and subsequently poured himself a large whisky, was he able to consider what he should do next.

'Tracey?'

'Jack, what's wrong? You never call me. What's up with a text?'

It was early the same evening. Jack had knocked back a couple of whiskies on his now too-empty stomach. His late lunch with Tracey seemed a long time ago. He was wishing he hadn't gone to Chasewater, and he really wished he hadn't found out the identity of the body, but he had, and he needed to work out what he was going to do with the information.

'I know, I couldn't just message this though.

Where are you?'

'Just getting changed before meeting Gavin. What is it?' Jack could hear his friend's concern in her voice. 'Is someone hurt?'

'I know summat about the bloke that died.' The drinks were having a disproportionate effect on him. He wasn't pissed, not by a long way, though he knew that would be his final destination that night. The drinks he'd already consumed had started to take effect. His accent was showing its stronger Black Country roots. He could hear it in his voice, and he could hear his mother's quietly berating him for it.

'What is it?' Tracey repeated.

'I'd spoke to him on Grindr, I know it was him because of the tattoo that they've found on the body'.

'Are you sure?' Tracey sounded doubtful. 'Couldn't you know lots of people who could have tattoos?'

'I'm sure it's him. There can only be so many men nearby with tattoos of the TARDIS on their arse.' He heard Tracey stifle a giggle. Dammit, didn't she know how serious this was?

'Do you have a name, Jack?' He recognised the technique that she was using on him, one used when questioning members of the public. Elicit as much information that you can from them, you can piece it all together later. Reluctantly Jack realised that this was why he had made this call to her.

'No, just a screen name: Marty McFly. But there's can't be that many people using that name in the local area, can there?'

'It's going to be a bugger to trace him with just that though. You sure you've not got any more information?'

'He may have given me his real name in my chat history, but I don't remember, and anyhow I've deleted it from my phone'.

Tracey swore loudly then continued. 'Why on earth did you do that?'

'Because I'm implicated aint I? I'm known to the victim.'

'Well yes, but that doesn't make you a murderer does it.'

'Can you pass the information on to someone, someone higher up? I know it's not much to go on but I'm sure he's the victim.'

'Leave it with me, I'll see what I can do.' She finished the call. Any brusqueness in cutting short the conversation hadn't register with Jack. He was simply relieved to be able to pass his problem on to someone else.

It was late. The drinking had continued. First the whisky. Then, when he'd finished the Jamesons, on to Bacardi rum with a dash of coke, each successive glass having less coke, and more rum.

Despite his best efforts to curb his hunger pangs, he ordered a too-large pizza to be delivered, arguing with the shop when they said that they were closing. Knowing him as a regular customer, and as far as they knew still a police constable, the owner agreed to drop it off on his way home after they had locked up. This meant it was barely lukewarm when it arrived, but Jack didn't care. He needed carbs and something to soak up the booze. He tipped generously which assuaged the grumblings of the shop owner.

He'd not been on a bender like this in all the time since he had been suspended. His self-control, with hindsight, had been incredible. But this Monday - well, Tuesday morning now, he noted - it had all been too much for him, and he was wallowing in self-pity.

He didn't want to switch the television on. At this time of night it was going to be full of crap shows and he didn't want to risk even a glimpse of a naked woman when flicking through the late night channels. Nothing he had recorded on his Sky Box held any appeal for him either, and radio just annoyed him.

He started flicking through photos on his phone. He had pictures there from over ten years ago, before he joined the force. The year-by-year view pictures showed him maturing through their twenties, following the various fashions for facial hair, like the face of mannequin in a gentlemen's clothing shop, zooming forward as in HG Wells' The Time Machine. Beard, goatee, stubble, he'd passed through them all until reaching his current clean-shaved look.

And the boys - or rather men in the latter years that he had his arm around. Some were remembered fondly, others less so, depending on the length of the relationship. A long, three-year stretch from around seven years ago with photos of just him and Russell, then just as abruptly as he had appeared in the photos, he disappeared. Gone travelling, scared of the idea of being with the same person for the rest of his life. What would the time be in Melbourne now? He hadn't drunk-sexted Russell for ages. Before his brain could engage, he sent a flirtatious text, a variation on the same one he had sent off and on every few months since dropping him off at Heathrow airport four years previously.

Jack was getting maudlin, and he knew it. He should drink some water and go to bed, but he knew that all he would do was lie there and think about 'Marty McFly'. Missed opportunities. What if they had met up? Sure, he was younger than Jack, but not by so many years, according to his profile anyhow. Jack, like most people, had shaved a few years off the date of birth of his online profile. He imagined settling down with Marty, in much the same way he had at some point envisioned he and Russell marrying. Jesus, he'd never even met the guy, and now he was marrying him. He was dead and Jack didn't even know his real name.

He threw the empty bottle onto the comfy chair opposite, bouncing onto the wooden floor with a clatter, his downstair neighbour wouldn't be impressed, especially this time of the night, correction, morning.

He was surprised when a WhatsApp message pinged on his nearly dead phone. He doubted very much it was his ex-boyfriend. Russell had never responded to any of the other texts or pictures he had sent him over the years. It was Tracey.

[You still up?]

[Yeah, haven't you got work tomorrow?]

[I'm still buzzed. The Detective Inspector rang me personally to thank me for the tip off about 'Marty'. He did wonder how I knew though. I played it cagey and said that it was a source who wished to remain anonymous.]

[Thanks]

[You OK?]

[Just a bit low that's all. He was a friend, a mate, you know?]

[But you never actually, you know...] The emoji of an aubergine flashed on his screen before being deleted. Tracey then sent through the emoticon of two guys holding hands, followed by a lipstick-smeared kiss. Jack was getting tired, both physically and of this conversation.

[I'm off to bed. Let me know if you find out his real name and glad you're a rising star.]

Jack put the 'Do Not Disturb' setting on his phone, though he could see Tracey was still typing away in response to his message. It seemed for all of his loneliness the last thing he actually wanted this evening was other human contact. He toyed briefly with the idea of firing up one of the dating apps on his phone, even to reinstall the Grindr app that had got him into so much trouble in the first place. But the booze and depression seemed to have gotten the better of him. He shucked out of his clothes, leaving them in a pile on the lounge floor and headed to the bedroom, forgetting to drink some water to prevent the inevitable hangover before collapsing on the bed.

The heat in the bedroom, despite the open windows was oppressive, and Jack lay naked on top of his sheets, finally slipping into a shallow and disturbed sleep. His dreams were troubled, the erotic memories of the few pictures that he and 'Marty' had shared came tumbling through his mind and he struggled to remember what had really happened in the relationship and what they had shared online about what they intended to do. Not much, he recalled. They hadn't even talked on the phone, let alone met up.

CHAPTER THREE

The next morning, Jack woke late. His hangover was in full swing, despite the paracetamol taken in the early hours of the morning when a raging thirst had woken him. Dried drool was encrusted the side of his face, and his tongue felt like a cat had used it as a litter tray. His head was still pounding, mostly due to dehydration but also through lack of sleep. Even though it was ten o'clock, he'd only really had four or five hours.

Still naked, he padded through to the kitchen, and drank a large glass of water. Taking more tablets and eating a piece of toast made him feel slightly more human. Like all too many days since the start of his suspension, he didn't yet have a clear plan as to what to do for the rest of the day. The feeling of guilt over what had happened to the lad he had flirted with online was still huge and unsurprisingly, he reflected, drinking himself into a stupor hadn't made his thinking any clearer.

A long hot shower, a shave and putting on fresh clothes made him feel slightly more human. As always, the drumming massage of water on his head helped alleviate some of the symptoms. The heat in the apartment was rising again. It looked like it was going to be another scorcher.

He checked his phone. The usual junk emails, nothing really happening on the social media accounts he monitored. As he held his phone in one hand and scrolled through his Twitter feed with his thumb, it vibrated, and a WhatsApp notification appeared from Tracey.

[They have a name for the body. Martin Barr. There will be a press conference later today. I did *not* tell you this. X]

At least now Jack had a name. He wasn't sure how this made him feel. Whilst he was 'Marty McFly' he was anonymous, just someone who had been in his life, albeit exclusively online. He didn't know the name. There were certain surnames that, as a police officer, you started to recognise: family clans in the local area where trouble was passed from one generation to the next. Most of this was low-level trouble, antisocial behaviour, drunk and disorderly, a little low-level drug activity. Barr didn't ring any bells.

Around and around in circles. Even knowing the victim's name Jack didn't seem to be able to settle. His first instincts upon hearing about the incident however were right however, it hadn't been an accident. Maybe he wouldn't be able to solve this, he admitted to himself. After all it wasn't his job, and the way the suspension and investigation were going it may never be his job again. Why should he be worried about it?

But he did have a connection with Martin. And at some deep level that he couldn't explain this meant that he was responsible. He wished again that he hadn't been so quick to delete the message history now, and he knew even though it had been deleted from his phone, it was still sitting on some company servers. That didn't make him feel any better.

He needed to know more about Martin. The number of times he could hassle Tracey and his former colleagues was limited, and he had already pushed her too far. He didn't want to lose what few friends he had left on the force.

He fired up the laptop and typed the victim's name into Facebook. There was a few Martin Barrs that cropped up, but only one in the Burntwood area. He clicked on the name to see what information came up. Some people were happy to share their entire lives online. Others were more circumspect. Of course, without a warrant and access to Martin's passwords, the amount of information he was going to be able to access was limited.

He clicked through, and a surprising amount of information was made available to him, even on a 'private' profile. He thought people were savvier today about sharing information. Some of the details he was already aware of. He knew Martin was a security guard - he recalled a photo that had been sent through to him a couple of months back, with most of a 'SecuriCorp' uniform on and a peaked cap. He'd always liked a man in uniform. What other information was there? He had gone to Chase Technical College. That was something he could have guessed, given where he lived. A few more photos, wearing more clothes than the pictures which he had deleted from his phone. One was taken at Chasewater a few months back. Snow was on the ground. Jack wondered who had taken the picture. It wasn't a selfie, but full-length, showing as much of the background as of Martin.

Ah, here was a bit that that was news to him. 'Security Guard at Morrisons'. There were only two branches of that supermarket nearby, in Burntwood and Lichfield. He must have had work colleagues, so all he had to do was question them. If he was an active police office with a warrant card and badge, this would be an easy task. But since his suspension his automatic right to nose around and ask questions, the part of his job that Jack had always enjoyed, had been taken away from him.

But, he wondered, how many members of the public, and more importantly employees of the supermarket, would in fact demand to see a warrant card?

He went back to his bedroom and opened the built-in wardrobe. Hanging up and unworn for over four months in an old suit bag, he got down his uniform. His black custodian helmet was at the foot of the wardrobe, much preferred to the peak cap that had been the fashion a few years back but offering less protection. Having had more than his share of half-bricks lobbed at him over the ten years he had been on the beat, he appreciated the extra protection, even if in these hot summer months it acted like a huge heatsink on his head.

He put the black stab vest on, and matching trousers. He was pleasantly surprised to find that he was still able to wear them comfortably. Both his regular running and the time at the gym appeared to have mitigated the more sedentary lifestyle he had recently encountered. The vest seemed very light. His handcuffs and extendable baton had been taken away from him. He was hoping that a casual observer wouldn't miss these otherwise essential elements.

One thing was missing from his real-life 'fancy dress': his Airwave radio. Looking like a huge mobile phone from twenty years ago, it was as essential to a police officer as an iPhone was to most teenagers. Amazingly, he hadn't been asked to return his old radio. He fished it out of the kitchen drawer. It was dead, they needed charging regularly, but he clipped it to his vest anyhow. Maybe they assumed that it would be obsolete by the time it returned, the technology was years out of date and should have been replaced years ago, but like many IT projects it was over budget and running late. He couldn't charge his radio, but at least he looked the part.

He looked at himself in the mirror before

he headed out. Was he really going to do this? Technically he was intending to commit a crime - the Police Act 1996 made this very clear, he recalled from his basic training. After so long out of uniform it felt almost like he was doing some roleplay. He thought back to the couple of times he had actually worn the uniform when he had met someone for a hook-up who knew he was a police officer and wanted to see Jack fully kitted out. This hadn't felt just as sexy to Jack, just really, really awkward.

With a sigh, he headed out to the supermarket. If nothing else, he thought logically, he should be able to get something for his tea.

Of course he couldn't just turn up at the supermarket in his MINI Cooper. Even though the police had cut back, most officers didn't arrive in their own vehicles. He parked on a nearby housing estate and walked through to the large warehouse-style supermarket.

He should have known of course that there would be other police there, and a quick scan of the car park confirmed that there were two vehicles, meaning a maximum of four officers. Of course there may be others in unmarked vehicles. Whilst he knew some of the cars by sight, there was always a turnaround of vehicles in the carpool.

He felt highly conspicuous in his uniform, just hanging around outside the supermarket, trying to catch a glimpse of who was inside. He retreated to the local McDonalds just a short walk away. Anyone passing would think he was just on a routine foot patrol, and the young lady who served him gave him a McFlurry on the house, which was appreciated. Jack sat by the window, looking out onto the car park, and most importantly the only route away from the supermarket.

Eventually, when the final dregs of the ice cream had been consumed, the two police cars moved off. He caught a glimpse of the occupants, as he surmised, two in each one - the times of the lonely copper were long gone in the West Midlands area. He didn't recognise anyone in the first car, but a brief flash of ebony and that unauthorised white shirt in the passenger seat of the second car confirmed that Alan was driving, a plain clothes officer in the passenger seat next to him. At least he wasn't still sweating out on Chasewater, Jack thought, as he slid down in the plastic seating, failing to appear less conspicuous.

A few minutes later, Jack strode into the supermarket. Confidence seemed to emanate from him as he approached the customer service desk and asked to see the manager, as if he had a right to be there, rather than acting the imposter that he was. He felt deep down that this was a mistake. Still, he was committed now.

A nervous, middle-aged woman approached. Dressed in a pale blue polyester two-piece suit, it still seemed like she was in a uniform similar to the floor staff.

'We've just spent an hour with the police.' Despite her nervousness, 'Gill', as her name badge declaimed, was clearly not happy with being disturbed again. Well, here goes nothing, thought Jack.

'Yes ma'am.' Where had that come from? He'd not called someone 'ma'am' in the line of duty since some minor royal visited Lichfield years earlier. Ah well, if obsequiousness was going to get him the information... 'I'm part of family liaison. I'm not directly linked to the investigation around Martin's tragic death, but I am trying to help his family by finding out a little more about him.' He hoped that the logical fallacy behind this - that if anyone knew Martin it would in fact be his family - would pass Gill by, and indeed it did seem to.

'I don't mind at all.' As always, when the innocent were faced by a police uniform, thought Jack, they fell over themselves to help. 'Though he wasn't employed by us, but a separate security firm. He's been here for years, though, about three years we think, though we don't have his HR record of course.' As Gill spoke, she took Jack through the back of the store to the staff areas, and finally a staff rest room. It was still empty, he suspected, from the official police questioning that had happened just twenty minutes previously.

'We would just like to know a little more about him, his personality.' The 'we' implied that Jack was working for some higher authority, rather than as a lone wolf. 'Who were the people he was closest to here?'

'Well, the other security guards, of course, but I can't pull them off the shop floor. There were two people that I know he spoke to a fair bit. There's Alison - he took some really good pictures of her wedding for her. They were almost professional level. And then there's Fish.'

'Fish?' Even with the current trend for giving children unusual names, this would certainly stand out in the class register.

'Sorry, his real name is William Bishop, Billy as we call him. He works on the fresh fish counter, so he has the nickname, er, Fish. From Billy the Fish. You know, Viz…?' Gill's conversation faltered as she realised she was over-explaining. Jack tried to give a reassuring smile. I guess there are worse nicknames, thought Jack, as he thought back to the cruel nicknames he had suffered with at school. 'Gaylord' had been one of the more moderate ones.

'Are Alison and errr, Fish in work today?' He knew that due to summer jobs the rotas in supermarkets were complex and there was no guarantee that the manager of a large store would know for certain which of her staff were on the shop floor at any one time.

But without a hesitation Gill replied. 'Yes, they both are. The other police took statements from each of us. Will we have to give statements again?'

'No, no, absolutely not,' Jack replied a little too quickly. 'As I said, this is a very informal follow-up for family liaison.'

Jack wondered if there was any chance he could talk to each of them separately, just to make a few notes. He retrieved a black Moleskine notebook out from one of his vest pockets. Hopefully no one would notice that it didn't look quite the same as the official notebooks.

As he waited for Alison to arrive, he looked around the restroom. Painted in what was no doubt thought to be a cheering sunset yellow, the windowless office was stifling in the heat. An old air conditioning unit was on the wall, but the dust around the louvres seemed to indicate it hadn't been turned on in years. The noticeboard had all the usual accoutrements: a faded poster of the Health and Safety at Work Act, a few postcards sent from smug holidaymakers, and the rotas for the coming week, along with a few crossings out and arrows indicating swaps. Jack was just trying to work out the abbreviations on the rota for Alison and Fish so he could ascertain their surnames, when the door opened, and Alison walked in.

A short woman in her early twenties, the shop floor uniform fitted her too-tightly around the waist and chest. Her complexion was florid, and he could tell that she had been crying. Jack was usually as empathetic as a Tory politician, but he could tell that she was upset. He wondered if she knew yet that it was most likely a murder investigation. Jack had all the standard training for this sort of thing, and delivering bad news to people was all part of the job. Nevertheless, he thought this meeting had suddenly got a lot more awkward.

'Alison, please sit down. Can I get you a drink? It's really hot in here.' He motioned towards the water cooler in the corner.

'Yes, yes please.' Getting himself one as well, they both sat down, Jack at the head of the large meeting table, Alison perpendicular to him. She gripped the plastic cup so tightly he thought the contents were going to spill. Usually oblivious to such things, he noted her wedding ring, tight around chubby fingers. That would be as good an opening as anything.

'I understand Martin took the photos for your wedding?'

'Yes, yes, he did. It was a couple of months back. It was a great day, we've been lucky with the weather this year. He had all the kit and everything.'

'You mean photography kit?'

'Yeah, two massive cameras, kitbags, flash guns.' Alison's Black Country accent was broad, and again Jack was taken back to his school days when he had been ridiculed for his own accent.

'And why did you ask Martin to do it rather than a wedding photographer? The cost?' He realised that he was probing much further than someone who was officially involved in the inquiry would. If he was conducting this interview as a police officer on duty, there's no way he would have been able to do this. Step back, pull back he told himself.

'No, not at all. We had plenty of cash to splash.' Jack glanced again and realised what was unusual about the wedding ring. They were usually solid metal, but this ring had a bright, sparkling jewel inset into it. He doubted very much that it was cubic zirconia, but rather pure diamond. 'But Martin was so good we gave him £500 anyhow, for his time and all the editing he did afterwards. You know, people like him are always so artistic, aren't they?'

'People like him?' Really, had he just travelled back in time thirty years? People didn't really talk like this nowadays, did they?

Alison must have picked up on the look that passed Jack's face. 'I'm sorry, I did explain to the other policemen. I don't think he'd told many people at work, but he was, you know, gay.'

'And you've told the police? I mean, the other officers?'

'Yes, yes, I have. I know he hadn't told his parents or anything, had he? This wasn't anything to do with that was it? You hear of all sorts on these dating apps. I know he used them, though I told him there were better ways to meet someone.'

Jack could feel the colour rising to his face. 'But he was a good friend?'

'Oh yes, he was my best friend from work I would say.'

'Did others know him well, too?'

A slight hesitation from Alison. 'Well, there's always Fish. They were very good friends.'

Jack felt he was missing something. 'Do you think they were ampere than friends?' This could make the upcoming conversation with Fish interesting.

'I don't know, really I don't. You'd have to talk to him yourself.' Jack could tell that she was getting agitated, and he knew that there was very little more useful information he could gain from her.

'Please, don't upset yourself anymore. And thanks for your time. Could you possibly tell Fish, I mean Billy, that I'd like to see him?' He stood up and walked towards the door to indicate that the interview was over, hopefully before she started crying again.

'He was a good boy, and so handsome, too.'

Well there was something that Jack could agree with, but he held his tongue.

Fish appeared nervous when he popped his head round the door of the staff room. Young, no more than twenty, and to certain eyes attractive. Jack had friends whom he knew would be drawn to the look they called a 'twink'. His white fisherman's coverall seemed too large for him, and his bowler hat would have fallen down over his eyes had his ears not stopped it from doing so. Jack quickly realised this would have to be a comforting chat, there was no way he could interrogate Fish and be heavy handed in his approach.

'Fish - I mean Billy?'

A small smile. 'I don't mind either. As far as nicknames go, I've been called a lot worse.' His voice was slightly affected, but he had straight friends who sounded more camp.

'Grab a seat and relax, please. This is very informal.' So informal, Jack thought, that he really didn't want Fish to mention it to anyone else, especially any other police officers who might come back and ask more official questions again.

'I've already spoken to the other coppers.'

'Yes, but rather than the investigation itself I'm trying to find out some more information on Martin for the family. I understand you were a good friend?'

Fish kicked his legs backwards and forwards. His hands were clenched in front of him, and he was avoiding making eye contact.

'Yes.' This wasn't an easy interrogation, Fish was clearly concerned about how much information he could share. How could Jack put him at ease?

'Did you ever go out together, maybe into Birmingham? Ever go to the 'Gale together?'

Even if someone was so far in the closet that they had a Narnian postcode, if they were gay, or even curious, and lived anywhere in the Midlands they would have heard of Nightingales. It was the club that had started the gay scene in

Birmingham more than fifty years ago.

There was no answer, and Jack felt more reassurance was needed. 'It's been a few months since I last went there,' continued Jack, 'but I hear it's getting popular again.' Apart from getting a pride flag out and waving it, or showing Fish his Aussiebum underwear, there was little more he could do to persuade Fish that he was someone whom he could confidently confide in about his sexuality.

Fish smiled. 'Martin wouldn't go to the 'Gale. It's too far for us to get back from easily and I can't afford an Uber at 4am. I've been with friends in the past, though.'

'So, where did you and Martin go, then?'

'There's a bar in Cannock that's gay friendly, and we've been there a couple of times.'

'Not Candi Canes!' Jack couldn't get the surprise out of his voice. This was a notorious venue, a drag bar only open three days a week. He'd been called to it a couple of times in a professional capacity. While it was a fully inclusive club, the clientele was drawn very much from the shallow end of the gene pool, and he would have thought twice about going in there on his own or even as a couple. The drag queens on stage and hanging around the bar had very sharp nails and were known to lash out at the slightest bitchy comment.

'It's a bit rough, I know, but it's the only place we could get to on a bus where we would feel, you know, welcome. We'd share a taxi back, though Martin would always ask to be dropped round the corner from his mum's house.'

'And that address would be...?' Jack pretended to flick through his notes. This was easier than he hoped.

'Royston Road, number seven.' Jack tried not to smile too much. Getting that piece of information had been much easier than he thought it would be.

'So, you went on a few - can I call them dates? With Martin? He was a lucky man.' Stop it, Jack, you're not supposed to flirt with potential suspects - not that Jack seriously thought that Fish could have meant harm to Martin. He struggled with the idea that Fish would harm, well, a fish.

'I guess you could call them dates, but we weren't going out with each other. It's not the sort of thing people our age do.' Jack suddenly felt very old. 'But we had a few drinks and, well, you know what I mean?'

Jack knew exactly what he meant.

'Did you ever meet his parents?'

'No, God no! They are real homophobes, his mum and stepdad, apparently. He never talked about his dad, don't think he was on the scene, hadn't seen him for years.'

'He wasn't out to them then?'

'No, absolutely not. That was one of the reasons we never became more settled. He wouldn't challenge them on anything. My parents are totally cool about it, even though it was a shock to them.' Jack thought about Fish's slightly camp mannerisms. He didn't think that it could have come as that much of a surprise to Fish's parents.

'Did you and Martin fall out about it?'

'He knew how I felt, but to be honest that was the least of Martin's problems. It was no big deal, honest. I know for your generation coming out was this big thing, and I'm sure his parents would have been mighty pissed off, but it's nothing compared to how his mom would have reacted if he'd been sacked from here.'

'Sacked... he was going to be dismissed?'

'That's what I'd heard. I tried to talk to him about it last week, but he was more obsessed about getting everything ready for last Sunday. He wanted to get some really good pictures of the races and maybe sell them on.'

'Who's his manager here? He's not employed directly by the supermarket, is he?'

'No, there's some bloke who comes round each day from a regional office. I don't know his name, but he gets here about two o'clock. Turns up in one of the security vans, always parks in a disabled spot, like he owns the place.'

Jack couldn't risk hanging around any longer. Odds were that someone who was attached to the investigation could reappear soon, and being around when the official team descended again would not be good.

'Can you do me a favour, Fish? If you see the supervisor in the next few days, can you ask him to give me a call?' He jotted his mobile number down on his notepad and handed the page over. If this had been official, Jack would have handed over one of his business cards, but he couldn't risk it.

'I'll do my best, but I don't get out from behind my fish counter when I'm at work. Actually,' he glanced at his watch, 'I need to get back now.'

'No problem, thanks for your help, and maybe see you in Candi Canes sometime?'

Fish smiled. 'Sure.'

Jack headed home, partly to nurse his still-lingering hangover, but mostly to satisfy a craving for carbohydrates. He didn't think it was in character for a uniformed officer to sit in a supermarket café, tucking into a Belly Buster Breakfast. Instead, he headed home, shrugged off his gilet and made himself the largest fried bacon sandwich he could physically manage to eat. Butter and brown sauce oozed onto the plate in a greasy concoction that looked so awful but tasted so good. He was just taking his last bite of the mammoth butty when his mobile rang. He didn't recognise the number on the screen, and wolfing down the final morsel, he answered, 'Jack speaking.' He had almost burped his usual greeting.

'It's Alan Elvis here. You left a number at the supermarket to ring you?'

'Ah, hello, this is PC Appleyard.' Another lie.

When had he become so good at deception? 'I'm sure you've heard the very sad news about Martin Barr?'

A grunt at the other end of the line. Something told Jack that there was no love lost between Alan and Martin. 'Yeah, I was told when I came on shift this morning. I've spent all morning on the paperwork.'

'Paperwork?'

'We offer a very generous death benefit package here, HR want to make sure all the paperwork is sorted, and his stepfather has been in touch, wanting to make sure that it would be made good, despite Martin working his notice.'

'He'd been dismissed?' Jack was maybe acting a little over-surprised, but Alan didn't seem to notice, too engrossed in his own administrative burden.

'Yes, last Friday. He was working a one-month notice period. I told this all to the policewoman who rang earlier this morning.'

'Sorry, different department. You know how it is.' Jack sighed in mock empathy.

'Well, I'm restricted in what I can tell you over the phone. Data Protection Act and all that crap.'

Jack had the answer to that. 'I understand, but the DPA only applies to living individuals, and unfortunately, as we know, Martin is...' He didn't want to say the word 'dead', but let the pause linger.

'Well, of course, and it is a Police Officer that's asking for the information?'

'PC24601.' Jack knew from experience that no one ever remembered the numbers, and the prisoner number of Jean Valjean from *Les Miserables* seemed an appropriate moniker to give himself.

There was another pause at the other end of the phone, before Alan continued, 'We had to dismiss Martin. We don't mind people being a little distracted when working - Christ knows it's not the most exciting or interesting job, nor is it the most stimulating environment either - but this summer, Martin took distraction to new extremes. We analyse losses due to shoplifting against the security guard on duty, and when Martin was on, the store was losing significantly more.'

'How much?'

'We're talking hundreds a week, and most of this happened when Martin was the only one on duty.'

'Did you talk to him about this, find out why?'

'Of course! We're not a cowboy operation. We went through the full procedure: verbal, written and final written warning. Martin couldn't explain it at any stage in the process. He kept protesting his innocence and saying that it was a coincidence. We can accept a one-off, and in Burntwood the supermarket tolerates a certain amount of theft as the cost of operating in this area, but this had been happening consistently since May.'

Jack made his excuses and ended the call. He was still trying to work out whether this had anything to do with Martin's death. It couldn't be suicide, could it? Guilt maybe about losing his job, and then somehow Martin had killed himself and then fell into the water? But that hadn't tallied with what Alison had said about him being there for the power boat race. Suicidal people don't spend the day looking forward to something like that, do they?

Suddenly a wave of exhaustion overwhelmed Jack. Trying to process all this information was all too difficult with the few resources he had, namely just himself. He didn't even have a massive whiteboard littered with photos of everyone he'd met and evidence as all good TV murder investigations had. He didn't even have all his notes in any comprehensive form, just a few bullet points jotted down in his phone. He headed to his bedroom and flopped down onto the double bed, still in the majority of his uniform. He wondered how much the official investigation had managed to ascertain, but after last night's drunken text exchange - drunken from his side, anyhow - he was reluctant to contact Tracey and find out what was happening. He could try and contact Alan - after all, he knew he was working on the case - but Jack's reluctance to contact his work colleague was more to do with guilt over the subterfuge he had just perpetrated.

More guilt, more disturbed sleep. He wondered how Martin felt about having a stepdad, and he sounded like a bit of a git too not to put too fine a point on it. Coming from a 'broken home' was a term never used in polite company (or police reports) nowadays, but Jack was of an age to remember it being used as a derogatory term in the playground at school. Jack's own parents had been devoted to each other; less so to Jack, who was an only child and had been born along very late in their lives. After a couple of drinks, it had been their standing joke to say he was a 'happy accident'. They now lived in a retirement village on the outskirts of Birmingham, and he rarely visited, not through any malice, he just had very little in common with them.

Whilst Jack had known from his early teens that he was 'different' from many of his friends at school, this didn't have a significant impact on him until his fifteenth birthday. His usually very uptight parents had reluctantly allowed him to have a party for a few friends in the family home, the numbers strictly controlled by invitation-only. They agreed that they would go out for the evening, a chance for a nice meal in Birmingham at Bank, the newly opened restaurant in Brindley Place. They would be on the last train back to Blake Street at eleven-fifteen and expected to see no partygoers on their return.

Jack and a couple of friends put banners

and a few balloons up in the lounge to give the pretence of a birthday party. He was expecting ten guests in total, enough to ensure that things didn't get out of hand.

But it turned out that those friends invited their friends, forwarding the texted invitation that Jack had sent on to others. By eight o'clock there were nearly thirty people in the house, and the party was spilling out in the warm September evening. The limited quantity of drink provided by Jack's parents (two bottles of beer for each person they had anticipated, plus a bottle of white wine 'for any girls that take your eye'), had been quickly consumed, and whilst some of his friends had indeed brought a bottle, others were less fortunate in having older siblings or accommodating parents able to provide any booze.

Jack was too worried about the numbers and the noise to be able to relax. His green silk-printed shirt, bought specially for the evening, was soaked through with nervous perspiration.

The lack of alcohol quickly became a self-correcting issue. By ten o'clock, all but a couple of mates had headed off to a nearby pub which, it was claimed, would serve anybody. The two who remained were playing Grand Theft Auto on the Playstation 2 in his bedroom. He could hear the music thudding through the paper-thin floorboards. In some ways, Jack was relieved that the party had been a damp squib. With his parents not due home for an hour or so, he had time to clean up and mitigate any damage.

Tidying the house with a black bin liner dragging behind him, Jack felt low. The idea that this would be his big 'coming out' party had failed to materialize. He didn't know for certain that he would have had the guts to do it anyhow, but in his mind he'd had it all laid out. Whilst there were rumours that there were a couple of gay people in sixth form, a couple of years older than him, he knew them only by reputation rather than from actually talking to them. It was still comforting for Jack to know they were there.

He'd noticed that the video game music had stopped upstairs. He knew the game well, and the relentless soundtrack that played throughout. He headed outside first to dump the bag in the wheelie bin, then closed the front door. His friends wouldn't have just left him without saying goodbye, would they?

He headed along the hallway and up the stairs, not furtively but without making any unnecessary noise. He wasn't quite sure why he was being so secretive - it was his house after all.

As he got to his bedroom, the door was ajar. There was silence in the room. He pushed the door open to see two of his friends lying side by side on his single bed, the game long forgotten by the look of it. Their t-shirts were discarded on the cluttered floor, and the flies of their jeans were unbuttoned. They looked over at him sheepishly, but not embarrassed at being caught. Jack gulped, transfixed by the sight in front of him.

'Wanna watch?' one of them asked. Jack wished he could remember their names now, but fifteen years later, he could remember only how the two lads had looked. One was ginger-haired, with deep green eyes. Jack seemed to recall the nickname 'Leprechaun', though his thick Black Country accent didn't have an Irish lilt. The other boy was tall, with black hair, and had the slightest hint of a treasure trail down into his jeans.

Jack often wondered what would have happened if, at that point, he hadn't heard the front door slam, his mum shouting in a falsely cheerful voice, 'We're home!'

'Get dressed,' he hissed needlessly at the two boys who were already busily buttoning up their jeans. Jack headed downstairs to greet his parents and checked that all was tidy, as per their expectations, and cleaner than his mind felt. They may have suspected that his nervousness was due to other reasons, especially when he loudly explained that he had been playing computer games upstairs with two friends who were just leaving. As if on cue, Leprechaun and his 'friend' came bounding down the stairs, said the briefest of goodbyes to Jack, and beat their hasty retreat.

Fifteen years later, this encounter, or near-encounter, was still indelibly marked on his memory. The confidence of those lads, older than him but only by a year or so, was incredible, and further reassured him that being gay was not 'wrong', just 'different'. Later that night, with a giggling mother who had drunk too much wine over the meal, and a stern but sympathetic father, he had sat them down and explained that he thought he preferred boys to girls.

They had taken his coming out as a personal affront to their parenting skills and had made it very clear that they wanted to know nothing about what he did in the bedroom, thank you very much. They were children born in the sixties and in theory should have been more tolerant, but the indoctrination of each of their parents, Jack's grandparents, continued in them. All four of his grandparents had been active in the Methodist church, that was how his parents had met after all, on a coach arranged by the local churches for Billy Graham's huge evangelical rally at Villa Park on a sweltering hot evening in July 1984. And although their own faith had lapsed shortly after their wedding, it was still deeply ingrained in them.

He was glad he had been able to break the mould and set his own path. He respected them, acknowledged that in many ways he couldn't have been an easy child to raise, and there was respect, but little love there now. His brother, well that was a different matter.

Was it the same for Martin, or did he have a good relationship with his mum and stepdad? What Fish had said didn't seem to point towards that, and just because he lived with them may not necessarily mean that they got on well but could be due to economic necessity.

Jack stirred himself, showered and dressed himself in grey shorts. He started to prepare something to eat. Despite having sworn only that morning never to drink again, he opened a bottle of red wine. Firstly to fortify the ragu sauce he was making, but then he had a glass whilst cooking, then another whilst eating the spaghetti bolognese, and a final glass whilst washing up. Before he knew it, the bottle was finished and in the recycling bin.

Feeling even more morose at his lack of self-control, Jack settled on the sofa with his laptop, the television quietly showing reruns of his favourite detective drama. The protagonist was apparently able to teleport herself from a Northumberland beach (with stunning views) to the pathologist's lab, then back to her home with the assistance of just a few melancholy chords from the accompanying double bass with a piano riff.

On the laptop, he called up Royston Road, Burntwood, the address where Fish had told him Martin lived. The official investigation would have had this information since that morning. There would probably already be a police presence there, and they were no doubt taking any material from Martin's room that may be useful: his laptop, phone (if it had been found), even his Kindle e-reader to discover his reading habits and to check he'd not been reading any extremist publications.

The house, as shown on Google Maps, looked modest; a small, two-bedroom semi-detached home, one of any number of identical boxes that had been thrown up by the large builders. The estate had been built just a few years previously, a mix of private houses, market-value rentals, and social housing. He wondered which category Martin's house fell into, and whether he'd been happy there. It was just a stone's throw away from both the supermarket where he worked and Chasewater. Indeed, they were all within a five hundred metre radius of one another. Martin appeared to have narrow horizons, in every sense of the word.

If Jack was going to find out what had happened to Martin, he was going to have to talk to the family. He couldn't see any alternative but to try and pull the same stunt he'd succeeded with earlier that day. If you were going to be charged with impersonating a police officer, then you may as well add 'on two separate incidents' to the indictment.

CHAPTER FOUR

The next morning, Jack woke early with much less of a hangover than the night before, and even managed to get outside and complete a 5K run before breakfast. He felt better for it, and as he put his uniform on there was a spring in his step. There was nothing to this deception lark. The forecast was again hot, though at eight o'clock in the morning it was simply warm. He wanted to get to the Barrs' house early just in case there were any 'official' police officers around. The impression he had gained from talking to Fish was that Martin's parents may not be particularly early risers, and he hoped that the element of surprise would be to his advantage.

Parking around the corner, again to avoid questions as to why a uniformed officer would be in a MINI Cooper, he strode round to Royston Road. It's strange how deception becomes commonplace, Jack thought as he suppressed the same nervousness that he'd experienced the day before.

There wasn't a car on the drive - well, not a completed one, anyhow. The shell of an ancient Ford Escort older than Jack himself was on axle stands, no glass in the bodywork and no headlamps, and the body itself was a patchwork of metal and filler.

He rang the doorbell, and the melodious refrain of 'You Are My Sunshine' could be heard inside. The house really was tiny, judging from the outside, like a two-thirds scale model of a proper house. Jack rehearsed his opening lines again and again in his head.

No reply.

He tried again, the electronic doorbell going through the whole song again for nearly a minute. He noticed a curtain twitch next door. If the tune was rousing the neighbours, surely it should be waking up the household. He tugged his cap at the neighbours and took the standard 'copper can wait all day if necessary' pose, legs slightly apart, hands clasped behind his back.

After what seemed like an interminable amount of time, but in reality was probably only a couple more minutes, he saw a shadow move behind the pattern-glassed window. There was maybe too much flesh tone for Jack to be totally comfortable with what he may encounter when the door was opened. Thankfully, the fuzzy mass resolved itself into a blue amorphous shape as the figure approached the front door.

It opened to reveal a man, taller than Jack and wearing a dark blue towelling dressing gown with questionable stains on its front. Even Jack, whose taste in men was as broad as it possibly could be, could find little incentive to wonder whether the man in front of him was wearing boxers under the robe. Skinny, unshaven, and with dark bags under his eyes, his face looked drawn. Was it due to grief, or could it simply be that he had been woken from sleep. He appeared to be in his early forties but was prematurely grey at the temples, and the rest of his black hair was unkempt and greasy.

'Mister Barr?'

'No, I'm Nick. Nick Whitehouse. Julie Barr is my partner, though.'

Jack was confused. He had assumed that Martin's mother was married. This was the sort of information that the real officers on the case would know. He would have to improvise. Again.

'I'm PC, ah, Peartree.' He'd taken his name labels off his uniform, leaving just the numbers on his shoulder lapels. 'I'm the local beat officer and thought I would take the chance to introduce myself. I just heard down the station, and I'm so very sorry to hear about your loss.' He tried to look past the tiny hall, but all that he could see were doors and piles of muddy shoes stacked on the floor behind him. No bloodied murder weapon casually discarded in an umbrella stand, worse luck.

'Yeah, thanks. I appreciate all that, but this is the first decent night's sleep we've had since Sunday. Can this wait?' His accent was broad Black

Country, Dudley, or Tipton if Jack had to guess. Distance-wise, that was less than ten miles from Burntwood, but it would still mark him as an outsider to locals who proudly called themselves natives of Staffordshire, even if it was by just a few hundred yards.

'Yes, of course.' Jack tried to keep his voice calm, but he knew he probably only had one shot at getting close to the family. 'But I really would like to have a chat about Martin. How's about I make you and...?'

'Julie?'

'Yes, you and Julie a cup of tea whilst you get yourself sorted. Then we can have a cuppa. I'm sure you've all sorts of stuff to do today. I'll be fifteen minutes tops, then I'll be out of your hair.'

It was amazing what people would do for anyone in a uniform. The authority that came with it could always open doors, even with people who would literally cross the road to avoid a policeman on the street. Jack felt that Nick was one of those people, but that didn't necessarily mean anything suspicious. Many people avoided interaction with the police.

With obvious reluctance, Nick let Jack into the cramped hallway, then opened the door to the lounge. The room was dominated by a massive television on the wall, eighty-five inches at least, Jack estimated. The only other piece of furniture in the room was a black leather three-seater sofa, pushed against the opposite wall. Pizza boxes littered the floor. Jack could hardly criticise them. In the same situation, he was sure that he wouldn't be too house proud.

'I'll go wake Julie. Tea, two sugars each,' Nick said, and headed up the stairs leading off the lounge. Apparently, he was going to take Jack up on the offer of making the morning cuppa.

The kitchen was in a worse state than the lounge, but at least Jack had implied permission to have a good mooch around the place whilst the kettle boiled, on the pretence of looking for the tea caddy. There was a drawer full of takeaway menus and surprisingly few cooking utensils. The cupboards were full of breakfast cereals, and a large, half-empty plastic tub of whey protein powder. He guessed this had belonged to Martin, remembering that in some of their message exchanges he had mentioned working on developing a six-pack, and had sent Jack a couple of pictures to show his progress.

Plugged into the wall were two mobile phone chargers, connected to their phones. Martin's parents were clearly of a generation where they weren't surgically attached to their iPhones. One had a pink protective case complete with bunny ears. He pressed the home button and a picture of Martin flashed back at him. The other phone had a cracked screen and no protector. Pressing the home button yielded nothing but some Uber notifications and a couple of missed calls from 'Bruv'. Both phones required passcodes, and he had the sense not to try and guess the codes, although Jack had now plastered his own fingerprints all over the devices. Ah well.

He finished making the tea, including one for himself. It's a hard-hearted individual who would throw anyone out of their house before they had finished their cuppa. Juggling the mugs and kitchen door, he returned to the lounge.

Despite the heat, Julie Barr was wearing fleece pyjamas, slumped on the sofa with one leg tucked underneath herself. With Nick at the other end of the sofa, this left nowhere for Jack to sit comfortably - he wasn't going to perch himself between them. He wondered where Martin's seat would have been. Rather than standing in the middle of the room, he lowered himself onto the stairs. At least it offered him a position of dominance in the room, being literally seated three feet higher than the others. The French windows at the end of the room were the only source of natural light, and motes of dust danced in the bright sunlight.

'Thanks for agreeing to see me, Julie. I firstly want to say how sorry I was to hear about Martin's death.'

Julie was petite, and without make up her skin looked blotchy. Her streaked blonde hair was lank and lay over her shoulders. Jack suspected that under normal circumstances, her hair would be tied back tightly, in what he understood to be called a 'Croydon facelift'. He was never good at determining the ages of women, but he would have guessed early forties, meaning she must have had Martin at a relatively young age, possibly late teens.

'Thank you.' Julie held her mug with both hands, gripping it tightly despite the heat that must be emanating from it. Her voice was almost a whisper. It was hard to believe that someone as attractive as Martin could come from such a mouse of a mother.

'I know you've spoken to others about this, but when did you last see Martin?'

'It was Saturday. He came back from work late and went straight to bed,' Julie responded in a flat monotone. This clearly wasn't the first time that they had been asked the question. They both still seemed in shock. Jack had been involved in precious few murder investigations, and he wondered whether this was a normal response three days after the event. To get further with this interview, he would need to ask something to get an emotional response out of either of them.

'I understand that Martin wasn't your natural son, Nick?'

'That's right. I met Julie when Martin was about five?' He looked over at his partner for confirmation of the date, and she nodded sullenly.

'Has his biological father been informed?'

'I don't know where the bastard is!' Julie nearly hissed the words.

'Could you give me his name? We need to

pursue all lines of enquiry.'

'This is nothing to do with him,' Julie replied. 'He's not seen Martin for years. I wouldn't let him near, the filthy-' She stopped short, and instead took a sip of her tea, shooting daggers at both Nick and Jack.

Let's see if an open question will get more of a response.

'Nick, is there anything you can help me with?'

'What do you mean?' said Nick defensively.

'Well, do you know of anyone who might have wanted to hurt Martin?' A loaded question and one that he was sure had been asked of them before.

'If you had known Martin at all, you'd know that wasn't possible. Everyone liked him,' Julie interjected before Nick had the chance to reply. 'This must have been a random mugging gone wrong - for his camera equipment or something.'

He paused before asking the next question. 'I didn't know Martin,' Jack lied, 'but I have spoken to some of his friends at work, Alison, and Fish? Billy?'

'That faggot!' Julie's declamation seemed shocking in the quiet surroundings of the family home. The insult took Jack back to his school days; he'd not heard it uttered in anger since then. 'He was leading my Martin astray. There's no way he was a bender.'

Jack tried to control his temper, but he

couldn't let the statement go unchallenged. 'If you mean gay, madam, then you should use that word. I usually don't mind whatever term you wish to use to define my sexuality, but there are certain words that it's best not to use in front of a police constable.'

The stunned silence that followed was only broken by the muffled noise of the television through the wall from next door. Nick stared at Jack's lapel badge, seeming to memorise his number. He slowly clenched and unclenched his fists, a well-known stress management technique that Jack had needed to use from time to time.

'Who is your commanding officer, PC608?' Of course he had his real numbers still on his lapel badge. Shit.

Jack blushed. Normally, this type of question wouldn't be an issue, but he had been rumbled.

'I think it's best I leave you to it,' he said, walking slowly towards the door.

'You've not answered my question. Are you really part of the investigation?'

'I really don't have to answer your questions.' An air of righteous indignation sometimes worked wonders. Jack fumbled with the unfamiliar lock of the front door, desperate now to get out of the rapidly escalating confrontation.

'I think you do!' Nick retorted but still made no move to get off the sofa. Julie watched the exchange with interest, colour rising in her pale cheeks.

'Get out of my house you queer!' she finally shouted and threw her empty mug at Jack. It struck his high-vis vest, the dregs leaving a brown stain.

Jack walked out, slamming the front door behind him like a petulant teenager, and headed around the corner to his car. The adrenaline was still pumping through him, so he sat for a few minutes and tried to compose his thoughts, safe in the knowledge that he was out of sight of the house. That maybe could have gone better, he thought to himself. He needed a coffee.

Half an hour later, settled with a flat white and an indulgent almond croissant at the Costa on Brownhills' High Street, Jack tried to reflect on why he had reacted so adversely to Nick and Julie. It wasn't the first time he had been called derogatory names because of his sexuality, and he doubted that it would be the last - not if he still had a career as a police officer. He was upset to think that people still used terms like those, though, and thought that way in day to day conversation. Especially people as relatively young as Martin's parents. What sort of environment was that for Martin to grow up in, knowing that he was gay?

Again Jack wished he hadn't deleted the messages he had received from Martin. He believed their exchanges had been innocent enough (as much as any message exchange on Grindr could be, he reminded himself), but maybe Martin had been trying to tell him more. Maybe he wanted more than sex: an ally. Jack was glad that Martin had Fish as a friend, and didn't think for one minute, as Julie seemed to believe, that Fish had somehow 'corrupted' him. Jack had many friends who were straight couples, but they hadn't 'corrupted' him into being straight.

Chasing the last few pastry crumbs around the edge of his plate, he wondered what the next stage should be. He didn't think he would be welcome in the family home again any time soon, and whilst Jack could go back and re-interview Martin's work colleagues, he couldn't see what the benefit would be. He had no further questions to ask them. He could go round to Chasewater again, but the chances of finding anything that SOCO – Scene Of Crime Officers, had missed was minimal. With the rest of the day ahead of him, he had few options, and the reservoir was only a five-minute drive away.

Finishing the dregs of his coffee, Jack's phone vibrated. It was Tracey.

[You idiot!]

[What now?]

Jack admitted to himself that he'd been an idiot several times recently, but what specifically was Tracey referring to?

[You've been to see Martin's parents. They are *not* happy!]

[Bugger. How do you know?]

[They've been in touch with the SIO about why a 'poof' has been round reminding them their dead son was gay!!!]

If his deception had reached the Senior Investigating Officer, then this could not be good. Despite the air conditioning in the coffee shop, Jack felt his skin prickle with heat.

[I was just going to Chasewater. Any chance you can meet me there?]

[I'm knocking off soon. I'll see you there in an hour, but you really aren't helping anyone, including Martin.]

Suitably chagrined, Jack ordered another coffee and croissant. If he had to wait an hour to undergo the wrath of Tracey, he may as well be appropriately sugar and carb-loaded for the onslaught.

Tracey and Jack met in the Innovation Centre, the only two-storey building on Chasewater, and the home of numerous small start-up businesses. The ground floor café that Jack had visited two days earlier was doing a roaring trade. The gallery space had a local artists' exhibition on, a variety of paintings in different media and of extremely variable quality. Tracey wore a light summer dress with a straw hat, her dyed red hair peeking out from underneath. Jack had also popped home to change. It was going to be hard to deny Tracey's accusations that he had impersonated a Police Officer if he was still wearing the uniform.

'Much more discrete, though if I spend any more time with you, Gavin is going to think we're having an affair.'

'Ha! Shall we walk around the reservoir?'

'Why not? It's a nice day.'

Stopping for ice creams at the nearby concession stand, they strode off in a clockwise direction. Now the police tape had been cleared, they were able to walk all the way around the lake, a pleasant hour-long stroll.

'What can I do?'

'About what?'

'About the fact that Martin's parents have told the SIO that I went round there.'

'Oh, that. I've sorted it.'

Jack stopped dead. 'What do you mean? How can you "sort it"?'

'I dropped a note to the SIO saying that it must be a case of mistaken identity. I said that you were with me and Gavin this morning for brunch at BJ Diner, if they ask you for details. I said he must have transposed the numbers on your lapel badge.'

'And he bought it?'

'Seems so. I guess he would think that only a complete idiot would impersonate a police officer whilst suspended awaiting a formal enquiry.'

'Thanks. And thank Gavin as well.'

'I will, though he always goes a bit funny when I mention your name. You haven't fallen out, have you?'

'Don't think so. I'll drop him a WhatsApp when I get a chance.'

Their conversation had taken them as far as Jeffrey's Swag, where the remains of Martin's body had been found. A few flowers had been left on a nearby bench. With his phone, Jack took pictures of the cards that had been left.

'Isn't that a bit morbid?'

'No, these are people that knew Martin - or at least claim to have known him. I bet the investigation doesn't follow up on these names.'

Tracey peered down at some of the sympathy cards attached to the tributes, rapidly desiccating in the heat. 'What, you mean from Alison and all the friend on the checkout?'

'Well, yeah. But look at what isn't there: nothing from his mum and stepdad.'

'It's only been a couple of days, and from what you've said they're not the sort of people to go for long walks across the countryside, are they? Even if it is literally on their doorstep.'

'But surely, you'd slip a friend or relative a tenner and get them to drop some flowers off if you knew that others were leaving flowers. I hope my parents would if something grisly happened to me!'

'Your parents! Really?'

'OK, I'm a bad example, I have slightly

dysfunctional parents.'

'Too true. Uh-oh.'

'What?' Jack followed Tracey's finger to where she was pointing. 'I'm only a humble PCSO, but isn't that a bouquet of sunflowers with a pride flag sticking out of it? I didn't think we'd told the press that he was gay. His parent's aren't going to be happy, are they?'

'Given the reaction I just got, I would say that's a big "no". Who's it from?' Jack was still looking at the world through his phone's camera lens and struggled to focus on the scrawled note. '"With love from FiFi and your friends at Candi Canes". Damn, what should I do?'

'What do you mean?'

'It's obvious, isn't it? If anyone from the press comes across these tributes, they'll wonder what our murder victim was doing receiving flowers from the only drag club this side of Hurst Street.' He was growing more agitated. 'But there may be a stronger connection than him popping in there for the odd drink. Should we take the flowers? Who's FiFi, anyhow?'

'That may not be her real name.'

Jack knew Tracey was trying to help, but here and now wasn't the time to explain the complexity of drag names and the personas behind them. He made a decision and reached over to take both the pride flag and the note from the flowers. Winding the flag around its tiny mast, he tucked them both into the back pocket of his cargo shorts.

'Happy?' Tracey watched the movements with amusement.

'Happy-ish,' was all Jack could commit to.

For a while, Jack allowed Tracey to talk, letting all the details about the wedding wash over him. Even though he was her Gay Best Friend, he couldn't get excited about the planning, and a part of him still felt this could be a big mistake. It was more than just the drunken fumble with Gavin - or at least, he hoped it was, he wasn't as shallow, was he?

'Do you know how the official enquiry is going?'

'I've no idea, Jack, I'm a lowly PCSO. OK, I got a pat on the back from the SIO for getting Martin's online handle sorted, but we're not exactly bosom buddies.'

'But there must be a feel for how things are going. It's the biggest crime we've had on our patch in years.'

'All I know is that they are taking their time getting the forensic evidence together. It's not going to be a quick job, the water and the propeller blades made sure of that.'

'Do we know which boat caused the most damage?'

'We're contacting all of the racers, but there were more than twenty-five boats out there. We don't have the resources even for a visual check of all of them. They've scattered across the country now, too, so we're relying on other police forces, and you can guess how much of a priority they're giving that sort of request.'

Jack grunted an agreement. He could imagine if the Met Police sent a similar enquiry through to his own force, where exactly it would end up in the priority list.

They walked on a little further, always with the water on their right, and the woodland on their left.

'Why do you like this place so much, Jack?' Tracey asked.

'You weren't born here, were you?'

'No, near Dudley. I sort of drifted over this way, then when I met Gavin, we bought a house over Chasetown way.'

'Well, this,' he waved his hands and tried to encompass the whole of the reservoir and country park, 'this has always been part of my life. See that climbing frame? The first time I had to have stitches at Cannock Hospital was when I fell off those monkey bars. And that picnic bench there - I left my clothes there and went skinny dipping with Donny Wright one hot summer when I was eighteen. He got out the water before me and nicked them all and took them back to the car.'

'So, you've got memories of the place. I could say the same about Jubilee Park.'

'Yes, but let's be honest, this isn't just a park. We're on the edge of everything here: the edge of the M6 Toll, the edge of Walsall, the edge of

Cannock Chase. It's a bloody amazing place.'

'Except when people get killed here or drown.'

'That was tragic, what happened in June. But yes, even with that risk, I think it's a great place.'

The walk was nearly completed, crossing across the dam that kept back the reservoir waters from flooding much of the town of Brownhills. It was the realisation, around ten years ago, that this dam was made of nothing more than compacted earth that had prompted a massive draining of the reservoir. The process unearthed an unexploded Second World War bomb, but not the legendary killer pike that was rumoured to haunt the depths of the reservoir. The subsequent rebuild had gone over time and over budget, nearly bankrupting the local council, who eventually had to pass ownership to the larger district council to complete the work. But on this Wednesday afternoon, there was little evidence of the massive civil engineering works that had taken place, and the water was back to its usual high level.

'Thanks for all you've done, Tracey. I really mean that.'

'You mean lying to a senior officer and providing a paper-thin alibi? The next meal out is on you.'

'For sure, and send my best to Gavin.'

They hugged, and Tracey headed to her car, making the appropriate hand-flapping gestures as she slipped in to demonstrate to Jack - who had been distracted by a jogger in the shortest of running shorts - just how hot the interior had become. Jack kept the button pressed down on his car key-remote, and the windows slid down to allow the interior of his own car to cool before he climbed inside.

He looked back over the water, finding it hard to square what had happened there just four days ago with the calm serenity of today. The most frantic activity he could see was a couple of dogs swimming in the water off the boat launch ramp, fetching a stick which their patient owner repeatedly threw out for them.

A distant whine broke his attention. Thinking that it was a dragonfly skimming across the water, he looked up to see a small camera drone whizzing just a few feet above the water. He had seen these before; indeed, the police had recently started using larger professional drones to monitor football crowds and political rallies. He traced the pilot to a child sitting on a picnic bench outside the café, controlling the gadget with a remote that was bigger than the aircraft itself. A phone was attached to a cradle on the remote, providing a bird's-eye view over the water. Jack started to wonder and fired up YouTube on his phone. Surely the official investigation would have checked?

CHAPTER FIVE

Back home again, Jack had another shower to try and keep cool, and settled down again in just his grey Aussiebum shorts, with a can of cold lager and his laptop. He was determined to see if anyone had uploaded anywhere any video footage of Chasewater from Sunday. This may be something that the official investigation had yet again missed.

A quick search on Google brought up numerous hits for 'Chasewater', but those from the day itself were few and far between. He guessed with Instagram, Snapchat, and other social media nowadays that most people would only share clips with their friends. Movies and photos were becoming ephemeral again, stored securely in personal clouds and on mobile devices that weren't accessible by others.

He aimlessly clicked on a few links that may have looked interesting. There was some excellent drone footage of the reservoir at various times of the day, but nothing that he could find for last Sunday. Just when he was ready to give up hope, he remembered that there were some websites whose content didn't regularly appear in regular searches. Maybe they wanted to be in control of the results themselves or didn't trust Google's algorithms for directing traffic to their site.

And there, on Flickr, was what Jack had been looking for. Sort of. A user called furryotter had uploaded some edited footage of one of the races. The quality was amazing, and running it full screen on his laptop, Jack almost felt that he was flying over the water. He became mesmerised watching the boats, tiny catamarans with hulls that lifted out of the water. They seemed like little more than engines and flashes of light, their pilots reduced to crash helmets and an occasional gloved hand as they struggled to control the machines around the corners.

The quality was fine on his laptop, but at the speed that the boats were whizzing by, he couldn't make out much detail - certainly not enough to identify individuals. He skimmed backwards and forwards through the video, but there was very little of the shoreline in view at any point. He needed more detail, needed footage from later in the day, and he also needed a recording that focused on the shoreline.

Clicking on the profile link within Flickr, he checked out some of the user's other videos and photos. Many of them were of a similar style and quality to the drone footage taken at Chasewater, showing different scenes in the local area, including Brownhills Common and Cannock Chase. But scrolling through the videos, there were some older ones taken not with a drone, but with a camera phone a couple of years ago. They were of people dancing to loud, thumping music. Clicking the video to full screen, he tried to focus on their faces, then something else clicked with Jack. They were all men, and he was looking at the dance floor of the Nightingale, the club that he had talked to Fish about only the day before. It seemed that the drone photographer was 'family', or at least was family friendly. The profile picture gave little away, a stylised avatar of an otter looking seductively out from the screen. Jack had little to lose by making contact with him.

He wondered how he might go about contacting furryotter and seeing if he had more footage. A quick Google of his nickname found him on various sites, and a few clicks later he had sent a message over to him.

Jack was pleasantly surprised to receive a reply within minutes. His experience of contacting strangers online led him to believe that it would be hours or even days before he received a response, if at all.

[Hiya, yes I do have a lot of footage from Sunday. There's too much to send over electronically and I've not edited or looked at most of it. I like your profile pic. Could I maybe come over to yours and show you it if you are local to Chasetown? Oscar]

Jack was taken aback by the direct tone of the message and wondered if he had met up with Oscar in the recent past. Whilst he had enjoyed a few one-night stands with the local population, given his job he was always wary of who he hooked up with. He could still count the number of them on one hand, well okay then two, and he was pretty sure that he hadn't met anyone called Oscar before.

[That's very kind of you, are you sure? I'm in for the rest of the day.]

He gave Oscar his address and mobile number. Even at this stage, he thought that Oscar might flake. But this wasn't a hook-up. Was it?

His phone pinged a couple of minutes later.

[I'm just putting some clothes on, will be with you within the hour.]

Gulp.

Jack tidied as much of the apartment as he could in the short time before Oscar arrived. This wasn't a particularly onerous task, simply a matter of loading the dishwasher, emptying the bins, and stacking the various bits of paperwork surrounding his disciplinary case into a single pile and stuffing it into the footstool. He had kept his cleaning lady on, even though he had plenty of time to do the housework himself nowadays. The fortnightly visit kept him in some sort of routine, and the bathroom and ensuite as clean as he, and his occasional visitors, needed.

Oscar must have been waiting outside because precisely on the hour he rang the bell. Jack buzzed the intercom to let him in without engaging in chit-chat - he was expecting a visitor, and a visitor had arrived. The internal doorbell rang a minute or so later, giving Jack time to check himself over one more time in the mirror. There were some advantages to living on the top floor of the apartment block. He took quick swipe at his quiff and checked his teeth to ensure he hadn't got any crumbs of almond croissant still stuck there.

When Jack opened the door, he was greeted by a man in his early twenties. Of average height and slim build, he sported a moustache and beard which must have taken a lot of maintenance and more patience than Jack had. Dressed for the hot weather in a t-shirt and shorts, his grin spread from ear to ear. Jack got the feeling that this was his natural countenance. Slung over one shoulder was a large and seemingly heavy laptop bag.

'Jack?'

'Oscar, come on in.' Jack directed him down the hallway to the lounge part of his open-plan living area. 'Can I get you a drink?' Jack was aware that he was hovering over Oscar like a nervous mother or a first date.

'Do you have a beer? I'm OK having a drink, I've not got to drive for a bit, have I?'

'Well, as a copper, I should point out that there's no safe alcohol limit,' Jack started to admonish a slightly shocked Oscar, but then grinned. 'But I think you'll be fine with one bottle. I'll get one too.' Retrieving the Corona from the fridge, finding a lime, and slicing it up all took time. When he got back to the lounge area, he noted that Oscar had kicked his canvas Vans off and rested his bare feet on the footstool. His thigh-length shorts had rucked up slightly. Jack might have very easily peeked to see what sort of underwear he was wearing, but he was trying to keep some level of professionalism. He chose to sit on the sofa perpendicular to Oscar. Jack realised that he was staring at Oscar, who held his beer bottle in his lap, playing with the neck of the bottle. The apartment seemed to become warmer, despite all the windows being open.

Jack motioned towards the bag. 'Is that your laptop?'

'Nothing gets past you, does it? Before we go on, is this official? Sitting here on your sofa, chilling and drinking beer doesn't feel very official to me.'

Jack hesitated. 'OK, I'll be honest. I'm suspended from the force at the moment, but the lad who died at Chasewater last Sunday, Martin, he was... a good friend of mine, and I want to find out what happened. And I some have time on my hands, so if I can do some work to help the main inquiry... I'm sure you understand.'

'How come you knew this guy - you said his name was Martin?'

'I never met him, just chatted to him on

Grindr, the dating app?'

'I've, um, come across it. I'm surprised. I don't think I've come across your profile on there,' Oscar said. At least that confirmed the suspicion, or was that now a hope, that had grown in Jack's mind since he'd seen the nightclub video clips just a couple of hours earlier. It wouldn't have been the first time that his 'gaydar' had been off.

'I keep a low profile, and no face picture. It's difficult with my job, or has been in the past anyhow.'

'Well this is very traditional isn't it, talking to each other in real life first.'

Both Jack and Oscar gave nervous chuckles and stared at each other. Rather than making Jack feel uncomfortable, he found it reassuring. He found Oscar very attractive, and he hoped that the feeling was mutual, a sufficiently rare event for Jack to find it both pleasant and disconcerting.

'Why are you suspended from your job?'

'I, ah, messed up on an arrest, got a colleague into trouble. It'll get sorted soon.' One way or another he thought to himself, remembering the upcoming visit with his Police Federation representative.

'So you're doing some detective work. I like that, I don't have a problem at all with you seeing what I recorded.'

'Thanks, it's really appreciated.'

There was another pause as they simultaneously took a swig of their drinks. In other circumstances the silence could have been awkward, but Jack felt very relaxed in Oscar's company.

'Do you mind if we get comfortable first though, there's a lot to see, and it's really warm in here.' Without warning Oscar removed his grey t-shirt, bundled it up and threw it at Jack playfully.

He revealed a slim physique, with more hair than Jack had expected despite his YouTube moniker, and a bear paw tattoo across the lower right-hand side of his body. He'd heard the body type described as 'otter' amongst his friends. Sleek but furry.

Jack sat their holding the warm t-shirt, he could smell Oscar's scent, which was not unpleasant at all. He realised that in comparison to Oscar he was ridiculously overdressed, and in his own home too.

Oscar smiled again. 'Do you mind if I take a shower, will help me cool down.' Without waiting for a reply, Oscar stood up and slowly undid the buttons of his cargo shorts.

'So, you were going commando!' Was all that Jack could manage to say.

CHAPTER SIX

There was the usual slightly embarrassed glances and small talk the next morning, broken only by acknowledging that they each preferred to spend ten minutes staring into their respective phones rather than each other's eyes. Oscar may have slightly spoiled the moment by suggesting 'round two' rather than a romantic reunion of two kindred spirits which was how Jack was trying to visualise the inevitable early morning encounter.

Half an hour later, and with coffees in hand and both of them propped up in bed, Jack returned to the reason for inviting Oscar over, before being side-tracked by his advances.

'Can we watch the drone footage you took at the powerboat racing?'

'There's an awful lot of it you know, we could be here for hours.' Oscar replied, with a grin on his face.

Jack sulked a little, he knew there would be a lot to work through, if he had the resources of a CID team, they would sift through it frame by frame. He wondered how he could shorten the time that this took.

'Are the files time stamped?'

'Yes, of course, you mean you don't want to spend the whole day with me in bed watching my amazing cinematography then?'

'Well...' Jack didn't know Oscar well enough yet to know whether he was joking about this or not. The post-orgasm drowsiness had also hit, something the coffee had yet to remedy.

'I'm not sure what I'm looking for, that's the problem, but it must be before the last race.

'We can look from about three o'clock then. I did a slow circumference of the lake just before the last race, so I could edit in as establishing shots.' For Jack, whose knowledge of filmmaking was limited to Instagram filters, this was just words.

'Will the quality be any good?'

'Yeah, 4K it's recorded at. Of course, the limitation will be what we view it on. There are only a few laptop screens that have got that resolution.

'Can we show it on a TV?'

'If you've got a HDMI cable, sure.'

This was turning into one of Jack's stranger Wednesday mornings. Lying in bed with a relative stranger, watching a video from an external hard drive daisy-chained to a laptop, in turn plugged into his bedroom TV.

Shown on the large screen the details were crystal clear. The bright sunlight meant that the water didn't appear a normal deep blue, but a bright shining silver. The surrounding land in contrast almost seemed dark in comparison.

Jack could see the boats racing around the course, guided by the orange, blue and white buoys in a complex pattern that the casual observer could hardly work out. Individual people could be discerned, a lot of flesh exposed Jack couldn't help but notice, and bare-chested men who could have been quite a distraction if he were not focused on the job in hand. He reflected on why he hadn't headed to Chasewater himself last Sunday, then remembered the terrible hangover that he had been nursing for most of Sunday, spent with a damp towel on his head and listening to the radio in bed, whilst feeling sorry for himself.

'Not bad, eh?' Oscar was rightly proud of his camera work. 'Four grand the drone cost me, but worth every penny.'

Jack agreed with him but was getting impatient. 'Can you skip to that final bit, you said you did a lap of the water?'

Oscar sighed, 'Hang on, I'll find the clip.' A few deft button presses, and a folder directory came up instead of the images. Oscar zoomed through to the 4pm timeline, there were two files.

'I did a slow clockwise then anticlockwise pan round the perimeter. Gives me choices when I edit it together.'

Focused more on the land than the water, the picture's contrast was improved, more of the landscape came into focus. Oscar had clearly dropped the drone lower than when he was chasing the powerboats round the water too. Some individuals captured on the film noticed the drone, Jack recalled that the few times he had seen the Police drones deployed they were far from silent, sounding like angry buzzing hornets. Some people waved at the camera as it swept past. Some, who had probably had a few more drinks than they should have in the hot weather, flicked V signs or demonstrated in the air their own masturbation techniques. Charming, thought Jack.

There was a small promontory where the footpath came closest to the water. Years ago, a small brick-built folly had been built there. Less than ten foot tall it was only known locally as 'The Castle', and generations of local children had made it their first point of call when visiting Chasewater. Recorded on the hard drive however late in the afternoon, there was just one figure on the Castle. Wearing a black gilet waistcoat and peering through the lens of what appeared to be a very expensive camera was a man in his early twenties, oblivious to the drone slowly panning above him.

'Stop!' shouted Jack, louder than he needed too. If his nosy neighbour was in her adjacent bedroom, she would be wondering what he and Oscar were doing. Oscar paused the playback. When froze, the picture lost some of its detail and clarity. But there was no doubt in Jack's mind. That was the last image taken of Martin alive.

'Have you shown this anyone else?' Oscar

was taken aback by the sternness in Jack's voice.

'No, as I said I've not had chance to process the film yet. The Flickr videos were just something I knocked together on the day and uploaded quickly, you know, to get some more likes?'

'Well I think once we're done here you should go home and give 101 a ring. I think they will be very interested in the footage.'

'Okay, that'll give me time to make a copy, I don't want them taking everything away with them.' Oscar was thoughtful for a while. 'This is big, isn't it?'

Jack tried to reassure him. 'It may be nothing, but they do need to see this. It's important that we know where Martin was leading up to his death.'

'But no one is going to do anything to him there. It's the most exposed part of Chasewater, anyone from hundreds of yards can see him up there.'

'That's true, so whatever happened to him must have happened later. Can we watch the last clip, you said it was going the other way round the reservoir?'

'Hang on a minute. It's about half an hour later, I had to change the batteries.' The same deft use of the remote control, and in seconds a similar view appears on screen. The light was softer somehow, this was taken later in the day and as the camera was pointing in the other direction, the sun was behind the drone, casting longer shadows.

A similar, if not identical sea of people passed in front of the drone. So many people, thought Jack, so many suspects. Cars were still littered around the nature reserve, some seemingly abandoned. There had probably been some structure to the parking earlier in the day, but as people had left isolated cars were left to be claimed by late stragglers.

'This footage isn't very good, I'll probably not use this one but the other one running backwards if I need some anti-clockwise film.' Oscar was talking about depths of field and apertures, things that Jack only knew in the vaguest of terms.

There was a white car making its way down the track at what Jack thought of as the back of the reservoir, near the sailing club. It was unusual because the track led nowhere, just a turning circle. Something drew Jack's eye to it. That was it, a massive Uber sticker on the side. The Uber number could be seen clearly. Jack made a note of it. As the car was heading parallel to the drone though, Jack couldn't see the occupants, or the registration number. The Skoda had tinted windows at the rear.

'Can you zoom in on that car?' Jack asked. Oscar paused the picture, framed it, and pressed a few buttons. The car filled the screen, but the detail was fuzzy, indistinct.

'Is that the best you can do?' Jack snapped, and instantly regretted it. He knew that American crime shows had given a completely false impression of how photo-enhancement worked. He was sure that a professional team with the right tools may be able to make out more detail. But Oscar, and he, were a long way off that. There was a silence, then.

'I think I'd better head off, I've got things to do.' Oscar was polite but clearly pissed off, and who could blame him? Jack thought. Oscar headed out of bed to find his clothes, which had been strewn around the lounge the night before. He came back into the bedroom buttoning his fly up and giving Jack a harsh glare.

'I've got your number, I'll call you as soon as...' Jack didn't know how to finish the sentence.

Oscar disconnected his laptop and started stuffing it into his Swiss Army rucksack. 'That's fine. I'm busy for the next few days, anyhow, and I'll call the police as soon as I get chance. Bye.'

Jack heard the jangle of his own keys as the front door was unlocked, then the too-loud bang of it closing behind Oscar. Yet again, he had managed to screw up a relationship before it even started, with another meaningless notch on the bedpost. And not even a goodbye kiss.

It was a while before he had the energy or motivation to get himself up, but with the sun streaming through the open window, he knew if he went back to sleep, he would wake up with a headache and still not feel any better about how he had spoken to Oscar. He made a note on his phone of the car details, all that he could recall. He wondered how he would be able to ever track down the Uber driver, and whether it was important to his investigation.

Wandering around his apartment, wondering what to do with the rest of his day, Jack found his food cupboard bereft of essentials and also remembered that his cleaner had left him a note saying they were short of certain supplies. The temptation to do an online shop and get it delivered whilst barely lifting a finger was strong, but the weather was still warm and getting out of the apartment would do him some good - better than continually moping on what an idiot he had been. Before he headed out, he stripped the bed and put the bedding on a hot wash and tumble dry, trying to expunge the previous night and morning's activities.

Like many small towns, Brownhills' High Street was struggling, of that there was no doubt. A third of the shops were empty, and those that were still open were hardly doing a roaring trade. But if you were not too fussy, there were enough shops and stores for most households to complete their weekly shop. These were helped - or hindered, depending upon your point of view by two big-brand supermarkets.

He strolled into town past the library and health centre, passing the giant stainless steel statue of a miner, officially called Jigger, but locally referred to as Morris. He first called at the butcher shop, then over to Wilko for cleaning products and toiletries. Before hitting the local supermarket, he stopped off again at Costa, sitting outside on the pavement to enjoy the weather whilst it lasted. It wasn't quite a Parisian café street scene, but Jack felt a part of this town.

As he sat and sipped his flat white, Jack carried out a mental survey of the row of shops opposite. Opticians, takeaway pizza restaurants, and betting shops abounded, and a solitary newsagent had been forced to diversify into a hot food shop.

In between tapping items of his shopping list into his phone, Jack watched the passers by. His eye was quickly drawn to a disturbance outside the betting shop opposite. Two men were arguing over something. Their muffled shouts could be heard over the noise of the traffic, though not the specifics of the dispute. Resisting every urge as a copper to intervene, Jack remained seated and simply observed. One guy, the largest, was wearing a green polo shirt with the betting shop's logo embroidered on the left pocket. The other seemed familiar to Jack. With a start, he realised that it was Nick Whitehouse. He still couldn't ascertain what the argument was about from this distance, but the betting shop employee seemed to be winning. He guessed Nick had been thrown out of the bookies' for some misdemeanour, and the ensuing argument had spilled out onto the street.

The shouting was nearly unintelligible. Swearing and with the odd pushing of the opponents shoulders with an open hand, but Jack had enough experience of brawls to know that this wasn't going anywhere. He thought that maybe one of the antagonists was drunk, but the more he looked, he could see that this dispute was fuelled by anger, not alcohol.

He debated again whether to intervene, not as a copper but as a concerned member of the public. That would have the advantage that he could more easily find out the cause of the argument. Before he could consider this option any further though, Nick separated from the other man and walked off towards the bus stop. He paused only to flick V signs at his former opponent, who was bent over double trying to catch his breath, the physical exertion finally catching up with him.

Feigning concern for the employee's wellbeing, Jack dashed over the road, closely avoiding being flattened by a truck on its way back to the local quarry. 'Are you OK, mate? I saw him do a runner.'

'I'm fine,' the guy wheezed, his face a vivid purple. Jack became increasingly concerned that the man in front of him was going to have a heart attack. The employee started to walk back into the bookies', and Jack followed. He knew the inside of a betting shop well, though not from his own gambling habits. His annual bet on the

Grand National was always through an app on his phone, but over the years he'd had cause to visit the shops a few times for disturbances not unlike this. Disgruntled gamblers whose horses had fell at the last fence had occasionally took their ire out on staff, and when patrolling the High Street it was always worth a visit to show your face. High visibility policing had been all the rage a few years prior before cuts to the budget had made it nearly impossible to maintain.

'What was all that about, then, Graham?' Jack asked, noting the name on his lapel badge. He tried to make the query sound innocent, but he also knew he couldn't press too hard. Jack didn't have his uniform to hide behind. He realised that he had spoken to Graham before, as part of one of his patrols. However, the betting shop employee didn't seem to recognise him, as often happened when people looked at the uniform, not the person behind it.

'That bloody scrote! He tried to ask for credit again. We can help out a little for our regulars, but that was too much!'

'How much was Nick asking for?'

'How do you know his name?'

Rats, thought Jack, so much for trying to build a rapport with the guy. 'I heard you shout it when you were arguing with him outside,' he lied.

'Yeah? Well, enough to make the manager take notice if it wasn't paid, and I've got no reason to assume that he would be able to make good. He works in the warehouse up on Lindon Road, no way would he be able to pay back four grand!'

I wouldn't be too sure about that, thought Jack, depending on whether or not Martin's employers come through on their death benefit payments.

Reassuring himself that Graham wasn't going to keel over from a heart attack any time soon, Jack excused himself. He wondered where Nick would have got the money to deal with his gambling debts if Martin hadn't been so tragically killed.

Jack completed his chores, headed back home, and put away his shopping like a loyal boy scout. He pondered what do next and ended up lolling on his sofa and flicking through the dating apps he had installed, more out of curiosity than with any particular aim in mind. Now that he knew what to look for, it was easy to spot Fish's profile on Grindr. The photo that was attached was of a bare-chested lad, cropped at the neckline so that you couldn't see his head. The profile name Billy_no_mates was enough to convince Jack that this was the right profile. He opened the chat window.

[Hi Fish, it's Jack here.]

[The copper?]

[Yeah, but I'm actually suspended from the force at the moment.]

[Since Tuesday? This isn't the usual way to

get in touch, is it?]

Jack sighed. This wasn't going to be easy.

[It's complicated. Can we meet up? I want to know more about Martin, and how he got on with his parents.]

[OK, you'll have to pick me up, though. I've not got a car.]

Jack wondered how this could look, a man in his early thirties picking up a teenage lad who he'd first met pretending to be a Police Constable and with whom he now had a chat history on Grindr.

[Have you eaten yet? I'll treat you to a meal at the BJ Diner. Send me your postcode, I'll message you when I'm outside.]

Fifteen minutes later, Jack was still unsure whether this was a good idea. But the deed was done now, and Fish was in his car, having picked the boy up from his parents' house in Norton Canes. He half-expected him to still be in his supermarket white coat and hat, but of course he was dressed as any lad would be in this weather: blue nylon tracksuit bottoms and a matching Nike sleeveless vest. It was a good job the diner didn't have a dress code, Jack thought.

Conversation in the car was stilted, divided between banal chat about the weather (still hot), and enquiries about work. Jack provided the briefest of summaries as to why he wasn't on active duty.

'That sucks, though. I'm guessing this guy

is alright?'

'Well, no, actually. He's probably going to be in a wheelchair for a long time, if not the rest of his life.'

'Shit, that's terrible.'

'Indeed.'

A quiet table was found in the corner of the diner, and the huge menu cards were perused, forming a literal barrier to communication between the two. Jack was surprised by how Fish re-started the conversation once they had ordered.

'It's about the photos, isn't it?'

'What photos?'

'You lot, you've found the photos he took of me?'

'What photos?' Jack repeated, though with the blush rising on Fish's face, he could guess what sort of photos they might be.

'They were just a bit of fun. I enjoyed posing and he gave me a copy of the best ones to keep - you know, for my profiles. He's got an amazing camera set up, really professional.'

'When was this?'

'Just a couple of months ago. Not long after my eighteenth.' Jack mentally breathed a sigh of relief, both parties were over eighteen. Even unintentionally, he didn't want to think of Martin involved in child pornography.

'How did you feel about it?' Jack asked. He didn't really have a moral view on the matter, and he was sure that there were enough photos of him undressed on the phones of individuals he had met over the years.

'It was fun, as I said, and kind of sexy in a way. I trust - trusted Martin a lot. I think I was his first live model, though. He seemed more used to photographing wildlife and still things.'

'I'm guessing this photo shoot didn't take place at either of your homes?'

'No, we did it up at Chasewater. There are some very private places there.'

That made Jack pause. Was this another coincidence? He tried to make light of the information and move the conversation along.

'That must have been breezy.'

'It wasn't so bad. We were nice and private.' A light flush started to blush Fish's cheeks, and he took his phone out of his tracksuit bottoms and started fiddling aimlessly with it. Classic displacement activity thought Jack, he didn't think he was going to show him one of the photos.

'Do you remember exactly where the photos were taken? It could be important.'

Their food arrived - the chef's half-hearted attempt at chicken Caesar salad for Jack, and a mammoth burger with fries and a mountain of coleslaw for Fish. Jack yearned for his teenage years when he had been able to eat anything without having to worry about his waistline. Fish had already slurped down a thick peanut butter milkshake and was waiting on another.

'I met Martin's parents. His mum didn't

have a good opinion of you,' Jack said as he played with his food.

Fish shrugged, answering in-between mouthfuls. 'I only met her once. I made the mistake of calling for Martin one Thursday. We were off to Candi Canes. Of course, we didn't tell her that. But we had splashed out on an Uber, and Martin had forgotten that his and his stepdad's accounts were linked.'

'So she thought you were leading him astray?'

'Summat like that. Anyhow, we passed it off. Said we were going to the bar next to the club, but we couldn't remember the name of it. She was angry, though, and called me a dirty poofter.'

'I bet that went down well. You know you can report that? It's a hate crime.'

'What good would that have done? Martin was having it bad enough at home without my size twelves getting in the way. I waited outside for Martin and never went back to their house.'

'Was his stepdad in the room whilst all this was happening?'

'Yeah, he was on his phone the whole time. Some footy match was on the TV. He seemed... I don't know. Zoned out.'

Jack abandoned his salad, and instead tried to slice and chew the rubbery chicken. 'Did you and Martin have a good time?' Jack hadn't intended to imply anything, but Fish's eyes widened.

'Saucy! No, we just had a good night out.

That was when we hatched the idea for the photo shoot. But to be honest, we weren't really each other's type. We were good friends, with benefits when we could, but Martin could never see us having a serious relationship. Not with his parents being so against it.' Fish paused and took a good long look at Jack. 'I knew I've seen you before!' He reached for his phone. 'What was your Grindr name? What Martin would have known you as? Here it is, Bobby_Dazzler. Bobby as in copper - very clever.'

'I picked it years ago. I'm not one of those guys that deletes and recreates my profile every couple of weeks.'

'You were friends with Martin. He mentioned you to me a few times.' It was Jack's turn to feel flushed. He wondered what else Martin has shared with Fish, if it included the less than artistic photos which he had taken one drunken evening? 'Oh yes?' was all he could reply.

Fish put his phone away again. 'Yeah, he said you were a really nice bloke. He really wanted to meet you, but he said you seemed a bit reluctant.'

'I'm ten years older than you, Fish, five years older than Martin.'

'That's nothing. I know for sure he wasn't bothered about that. Besides, from what he told me he was looking forward to meeting up with you eventually. You never...' Fish made eye contact with Jack then tilted his head to one side. 'You know?'

'No, we never… you know,' Jack replied.

Fish had polished off the burger and chased the last few chips around his plate with a fork. 'That's a pity. You could have been good for him, and you would have stood up to his parents, too. Better than I did.'

'It wasn't your battle to fight. Do you know what happened to the pictures he took of you? There's no chance Julia or Nick could have seen them, is there?'

'I don't know. He sent me them to me via WhatsApp, so they'd be on his phone, I guess? I know he had a laptop, and some way of copying the pics from the camera to somewhere secure.'

Jack reflected. Would he be that blasé if there were naked pictures of him sitting on a murder victim's computer?

'The police would have taken anything like a laptop or tablet for forensic examination. No one has mentioned cameras to me. I'll see if I can find out what happened to his stuff.'

'His cameras were really expensive, top of the range stuff. Most of his salary went on the gear. He told me if he sold them, he'd be able to put a deposit on a flat. He was looking around, that much I know. But he was sort of tied into helping his mum financially. They wouldn't be able to afford their house if he moved out.'

No-one had mentioned cameras to Jack. Did anyone else know about them, he wondered.

With the meal finished and Fish sated, it seemed as good time as any to head back. Jack asked if there was anywhere he could drop Fish off.

'You not joining us for a night out?' Fish asked. 'Me and a couple of the lads thought we'd raise a toast to Martin. It's what he would have wanted.' Jack raised an eyebrow. 'Well, OK, maybe not what he would have wanted, but we're doing it anyway.'

In the end, Jack agreed to loop round to Cannock and drop Fish off at Candi Canes just as the place was opening up. It was out of Jack's way, but he didn't mind. Fish was personable enough and had given Jack the only leads he had so far in what he was now thinking of as 'his' investigation.

'Look after yourself, Fish.' Jack passed his number onto him on a slip of paper. 'Drop me a message if you hear anything that might be of interest.'

'Will do, and thanks for the lift.' With that, Fish disappeared into the bar without a backwards glance.

Jack started making his way back home through the early dusk, wondering what had happened to Martin's camera equipment and the photos of Fish that had been taken with it. Whilst mentally on autopilot, he mused upon the confidence that Fish exuded, contrasting them to his own, hesitant experiences when he first started recognising that his own sexuality was different from many of his friends, nearly half a lifetime ago.

CHAPTER SEVEN

The next morning, Jack woke at what he still thought of as too early. 'Sparrow's cough', as his parents used to call it. He got himself ready for another day of... what? Whilst his suspicions about Martin's murder had developed over the last couple of days, there was no way the police would do anything about his hunches, and he had no formal way of passing on his concerns. Tracey had already gone way above and beyond the call of duty to provide him with an alibi for his last encounter with Martin's family. Jack was confident, too, that they would have investigated Martin's mother and stepdad thoroughly, and they must have cast-iron alibis.

But he couldn't help but remember the way that they had spoken to him. The homophobia from within the household was deep-seated. This wasn't the anger that he had seen often when dealing with grieving relatives, often directed at the police or someone else in authority. No, this hatred they showed for Martin was visceral even though he was dead, and exclusively because of his sexuality. They knew he was gay, and they were not tolerant of that. However, they must have been desperate for him to stay at home, otherwise they could not afford to keep the house on, according to Fish. How much anger would it take to turn that hate into something more?

He needed to get evidence to support his theory - well, OK, his hunch. He needed to find out exactly where Nick and Julie were when their son was killed. He had called in all the favours that he could from his friends in the force, so he was on his own.

He knew much of the information he needed would be on either Nick or Julie's mobile phones. People lived their lives through their mobiles, Jack included. He was sure that there would be some useful information if he could get hold of either of them. He also knew that the police would have already taken each of their phones and cloned their contents.

Jack's other lead came through Oscar, who despite him sending a couple of texts had remained obstinately silent. Jack had apologised for his behaviour the morning before, and there was little else he could do. But he was still grateful to Oscar for providing the drone footage with the Uber taxi, and the number on the side of the Skoda, but he didn't know what else he could do with the information yet.

Jack's first visit of the day was to the Grangemouth Garden Centre, where Martin's mother worked. One of the few independent nurseries left, it was well known in the area. Over the years, it had developed from primarily selling flowers, seeds, and plants, to these being almost incidentals. The café brought in more money than plant sales, and much of the rear of the centre was now franchised out to various small businesses, including a hot tub company, a microbrewery, and a vintage sweet shop. The exterior of the garden centre was surrounded by a dozen different sheds and log cabins, their wares permanently discounted, battling as always against the online retailers.

Jack pulled into the car park, but was hesitant to leave his car, despite the sweltering heat. The last time he had confronted Julie it had not gone well, and he was unsure what sort of reception he would get here in her workplace. He was not purposely disguised but wore loose cargo shorts and a polo shirt. With a baseball cap and dark sunglasses, he hoped that he wouldn't draw attention to himself.

He started by skulking around the potted plants and succulents at the front of the store, trying to spot any of the staff in their bright purple polo shirts. There seemed to be no staff around in the main foyer apart from a rather cute redhead youth wearing shiny black trousers that were too tight for him. He was lackadaisically pushing a broom around, while two women on the tills caught up on the latest exploits of the previous night's episode of *Love Island*.

Maybe it was too soon, thought Jack. After all, her son had only been killed five days ago. He didn't think he would have been able to return to work so quickly after such an experience. But then again, he wasn't working a zero-hour contract, meaning no work, no pay. The finances in the Barr household must be stretched to the limits, with Nick deep in debt and this job couldn't pay much more than the minimum wage. Martin's death benefit would solve many issues for the family, at least in the short term.

Jack was brought out of his revery when he spotted a shock of blonde hair, which as he had predicted on their first meeting, was tied back tightly. There she was, not in the main garden centre, but working in the café, refilling a cake stand with cheese scones. Unsure what he had expected to see, Jack was surprised to note that Julie Barr seemed very relaxed. She was smiling to herself and occasionally shouted through to someone in the kitchen. Moving to the café area, Jack picked up a tray and worked his way slowly around the chiller cabinets.

As he hoped, Jack could see Julie's phone bulging in her apron pocket. Having got this close, however, he had no idea how he was going to get hold of the blasted thing. He needed to improvise.

Jack went over to the soft drinks dispenser with his tray and filled four large paper cups with fizzy soda. He placed them carefully on the edge of the tray, and quietly moved up right behind Julie, who was standing on the customer side of the counter, arranging slices of cake to be self-served later.

'Excuse me!' he said loudly in Julie's ear, badly faking a Scottish accent.

As expected, Julie jumped out of her skin, and with the tray of drinks so close behind her, she didn't have time to adjust her movements before the Coke and lemonade spilled all over her apron and skirt. The drinks went everywhere. Maybe he had overdone the liquids a little. Swearing under her breath, she hardly noticed who had caused the accident. She took off her apron and bundled the sticky, damp mess onto the counter, before removing the other layers that had been soaked through. Without even looking up, she dashed out the back.

Jack did a good job of seeming to gaze helplessly around for assistance. Whilst there were people staring at the disturbance, they were all focused on the retreating Julie and the sticky mess on the floor. It was a work of moments to slide Julie's apron into the plastic hand basket he had picked up as he entered the store. As people came out of the kitchen with mops and cloths to wipe down the surfaces, he brushed away any offers of help himself and retreated to the toilets. Brazenly ignoring the 'no hand baskets' sticker on the door to deter shoplifters, he entered the gents' and locked himself in one of the cubicles.

He unwrapped the black apron, and there it was: Julie's mobile phone, sticky with the residue of the spilled Cola. Fortunately, it was a recent model that was waterproof, or at least splash proof. A quick rinse under the washbasin taps and it was good as new. He tapped the screen to activate it and was presented with 'Enter Passcode'. Like most people, Julie had password protected her phone.

Bugger.

Whilst he had Julie's phone, useless though it was without the passcode, hope still sprang eternal in Jack's mind. At least he had a good idea where the stepfather might be.

He drove into town and walked down the High Street to the betting shop that he had seen Nick thrown out of the day before. Sure enough, on the low tables in the centre of the shop, where copies of the *Racing Post* and the sports pages of the tabloids still dominated, Jack could see Nick seated with his back to the entrance. Slumped over and huddled over his phone, he was staring at something intently. The latest racing odds, no doubt.

Behind the security screens at the rear of the shop, a wary Graham acknowledged Jack's presence with an uncertain wave. Jack ignored the greeting. He didn't want to arouse Nick's suspicions any further. He wondered how aggressive Nick would be if he was confronted.

There was only one way to find out.

'Nick?' He turned around in his chair and looked up at Jack, who had deliberately placed himself inside Nick's personal space. Nick still had his phone in his hand. Jack rather naively assumed that he would be looking up sporting forms, but as he glimpsed the phone's screen, he saw a picture of naked women, legs spread. He didn't need to look at the specifics to recognise a porn website. 'Can I sit down?'

'It's a free country, can't stop you.' The look indicated, however, that Nick wished that he could.

Jack dragged a chair over and sat perpendicular to Nick, close enough again to make him feel uncomfortable. 'I just wanted to apologise for my behaviour on Wednesday, when I came round to your home.'

Nick looked up and stared at Jack's face. Jack saw the moment of recognition that casually dressed man with whom he was talking was the guy who had impersonated a police officer two days before.

'Oh fuck off,' was Nick's considered reply. 'Why are you hassling us? Isn't it enough that Julie has lost Martin?' Nick's belligerence was tangible, but at least he had put his phone down on the melamine tabletop. Jack didn't want to compete for his attention with the best that PornHub could offer.

'I know, and I truly am sorry. I just want to

get to the bottom of what happened.'

'Are you some sort of investigator? Have Martin's employers set you onto us?'

'Why would you think that?' This was something Jack hadn't even considered.

Nick sighed, 'They're challenging the death benefit, trying to wriggle out of it. I... I mean, Julie really could do with that cash. It will go a long way to help.'

Jack recalled his conversation with Nick's manager Graham from the day before. He knew that the police death in service benefit was significant, four times his annual salary. For a security guard, it may not be as generous, but even so, it would be worth thousands to Julie and Nick.

The phone was still sat on the table, tantalisingly close. If only he could distract Nick for a short while.

Fortunately, he didn't need to pour any soft drinks down Nick's trousers. From the other end of the betting shop came a loud roar. As one, all the customers turned towards the disturbance. Graham had closed the shutters on the secure till and was waving a fist at the punter on the other side of the reinforced glass. Jack couldn't work out what the argument was about, and it didn't really matter, as it had Nick's total concentration. He took the opportunity to casually reach over, and in one smooth motion, took the phone from the table and slipped it into his pocket.

Nick's gaze returned to Jack, and they tried

to out-stare each other. Jack looked away first.

'If you're not part of any official investigation then I'm going to ask you politely to piss off, again.' Nick's request was stated emphatically and given that he had a stolen phone in his trouser pocket, Jack was more than happy to comply.

With the punter still ranting at Graham behind the safety of the security screen, Jack pushed his chair back and left the betting shop calmly. As soon as he was outside, he proceeded at pace down the High Street and back to his car, hoping Nick hadn't yet noticed that his phone had been stolen.

Back in his apartment, Jack placed the two phones side-by-side on his office desk. Julie's was in a pink Hello Kitty case, and Nick's was without a case, unusual in itself. As expected, the second phone he had 'liberated' had a passcode, too. He had known that simply having the phones wouldn't be enough. He needed to access the material on them. He also knew that most phones would lock permanently or even wipe all information on them after several unsuccessful tries.

Of course, if he had the full police forensics team and a digital lab at his disposal, or even a warrant to force Nick and Julie to provide the passcodes, he would be home and dry. He wondered, in fact, why they still had their phones, and they hadn't been requisitioned by the force. If they had been cloned, as Nick assumed, it would be standard practice to confiscate their devices, even if they hadn't been identified as suspects. Message exchanges between the victim and their family could tell an investigation more about their relationship than anything that the relative said. Of course, people had the right to refuse this 'digital strip search' as the more extreme newspapers had called it, but that in itself could be seen as suspicious behaviour. Who wouldn't want to do all they could to capture a son's killer?

He continued to stare at the two phones. They stared back at him. Just then, his own phone chirped. Almost subconsciously, he glanced at it. The notification told him that, once again, he was overdrawn at his bank. Time to transfer money from his dwindling savings account. Whilst he was suspended on full pay, this was only Jack's basic entitlement, and he was missing the overtime and all the other additional payments that normally supplemented his police officer's salary.

Then Jack realised that he hadn't had to touch his screen to see the overdrawn notification. It had had come through, and the first twenty or so characters of the text had been shown whilst the phone was locked. He knew buried in his phone there was a setting that changed what was displayed on any notifications, but he'd never changed them from the original settings. He wondered whether Nick or Julie had bothered.

He pressed the home button on Julie's phone. Nothing. Swiping down and swiping to the side revealed blank screens. However, pressing 'home' on Nick's handset brought a whole screenful of notifications. Jack recognised the icons of a couple of betting apps, one of which was the same as the bookies' Nick had been in less than an hour earlier. Only the first few characters were visible, but they did not make good reading.

[Your account is in debit by £1839.65]

When the fun stops, stop. There were two pages full of these notifications. None of them had been read by Nick. As Jack scrolled down, though, he saw another notification which had a different icon. Black background with white lettering. Uber.

[Your Uber driver Mohammed will arrive in Skoda Octavia, BP67...]

The rest of the registration mark wasn't shown. He looked at when the message had come through. It was Sunday. He quickly took out his own phone and took a picture of the screen.

Nick had called an Uber on Sunday, of the same model of car that he had seen at Chasewater with the help of Oscar's drone on the day that Martin had been killed.

Jack knew that there was little else he could do with the phones as they were. He had all the evidence that his limited resources could provide. Now he had three options and weighed each of them up: destroy them, throw them, or return them to their owners. Chucking them into the local canal would certainly put them beyond use, no matter good their waterproofing, but would also mean their batteries would eventually leach into the water. Besides, whilst he had been unable to unlock them, others may be able to if they were found. He could simply drop them somewhere in the garden centre and the betting shop. Their respective owners may be reunited with them, or more likely a passing yob would take them to CEX and get fifty quid for each. In the end, he decided to take the least sensible option.

CHAPTER EIGHT

Well this was going to be one of the stranger calls Jack had made in his life, but there was no point putting it off.

'Hi Fish.'

'Jack, I didn't expect to hear from you again? Have you found out what happened to Martin?'

'No, not quite, though I think I'm maybe getting a bit closer.' A pause. Fish, I need your help, I need to talk to someone at Candi Canes, and to be honest I feel a bit weird going in there on my own.'

'And you want me to go with you?' his incredulity couldn't be hidden from his voice. 'This isn't a put up for you and me to be going on a date, is it?'

'No! Not at all.' Jack genuinely hadn't considered this as an option, Fish was too much of a twink for his tastes, even without the complications of the relationship between himself and Martin. 'I just need to talk to someone called Fifi there, I think she was closer to Martin than people knew.'

'I know Fifi, she, or rather he's one of the old

Queens there. I know her to say hello to anyhow. OK, it's a date, but you're buying the drinks.'

They confirmed the arrangements, and agreed to meet later that evening, the bar not opening until 9pm, the time that Jack was usually starting to look at his watch and making obvious yawning noises when out with his friends. Before they entered, they discussed their strategy as they walked the few hundred yards from the car park to the bar.

'You don't talk to anyone without my say so?'

'Agreed.'

'We're not dating.'

'Agreed.'

'And you're absolutely not going to show me up if any of my friends are here.'

'Agreed.'

So far this all felt a little one-sided to Jack, but he was aware that Fish was doing him a huge favour. He didn't know whether this was going to get anywhere, but it was the only thing that he had at the moment. Besides, he felt that he owed him at least a couple of drinks for the information he had provided, and he did like a decent drag act. Of course, the key word there was decent.

Fish had already fallen in with a group of friends, leaving Jack on his own at the bar, nursing the two drinks. Whilst no stranger to gay bars, there was a reason why he'd avoided Candi Canes except in a professional capacity.

'Hello handsome, is that for me?'

Jack turned to find a drag queen smiling at him. Older than him by around twenty years, he couldn't help but be impressed by the standard of make-up and the wig. Whilst the red sequinned dress was a little over the top, without them the drag queen could probably have passed for a woman of a similar age were they to walk down the average street.

'Errr.' For once in his life Jack was lost for words. With just a moment's hesitation, the drag queen took Fish's drink from him and started sipping it, just at the moment that Fish broke off from his group of friends and headed over.

'Hey Jack, where's my drink? I see you've met Fifi then?'

'I'm so sorry Fish, I had a raging thirst on me, I'm sure Jack won't mind getting you another.'

Left with little choice, Jack bought another vodka and Red Bull, still nursing his own tonic water. But at least he had now met the near-infamous Fifi, and albeit unintentionally bought her a drink. That must mean some sort of social obligation at least.

'Fifi, my name is Jack. I saw your floral tribute to Martin up on Chasewater.'

Fifi flashed an insincere smile at Jack. 'It was the least I could do, I knew his Dad wasn't going to be able do anything for him.'

'You mean Nick?'

'Not that bastard, his real Dad, Benjamin.

He and I had a bit of a thing way back when.'

This was a lot for both Jack and Fish to process, whose mouth was gaping like his namesake.

'You're saying Martin's biological Father was...'

'Queer as you and me, well as me Duckie, I don't know about you.'

'I do,' volunteered Fish.

Fifi gave Jack an appraising look, and he must have passed muster.

'Well Benjamin and I had a bit of a thing way back when, after he'd separated from Martin's mother of course. I'm no splitter of families me. But eventually the bright lights of London called him, and he buggered off down there, must be fifteen years ago, and we lost touch, I don't even have a number or email address for him now. If I had I would have let him know about Martin, but I tried to keep an eye on him.'

'Like a fairy godmother?' interjected Fish.

'Something like that. I've got to go, get ready for my show, was great to meet you Jack, hopefully see you again, when we've both got less on?'

With that she planted a kiss on Jack's forehead, leaving a huge lipstick mark which Jack was unaware of for the rest of the night.

'She's quite the...' Jack didn't know quite how to finish the sentence.

'I know.' Fish replied. I've known her a

couple of years now and think of her as both the Uncle I would never want and the Auntie I wish I had.'

'She cares for you, I can tell though, and for Martin.'

'Yeah, it was nice to have someone looking out for us.' To Jack's horror he saw that Fish's face was starting to crumple, and tears were forming.

'It's not fair is it?' Fish sobbed and Jack grabbed some of the napkins from the bar dispenser and passed them on, trying to stem the tears and snot.

'No, it's not, and I know the police are doing their best, but I'm also trying my hardest to see who might have done this to Martin.'

Fish started to compose himself, probably aware that some of the regulars at Candi Canes were starting to stare.

'How about I get you home, I don't think either of us are in the mood to see Fifi's show are we?' Putting a reassuring arm around his young friend, they slid off the bar stools and headed out of the bar.

Jack needed to talk to someone about what he had discovered. The case he was building up on who had killed Martin was convincing him, but maybe he had made a mistake. Every Vera Stanhope had a Joe Ashworth. Every Sherlock Holmes had a John Watson. Jack Appleyard had...

'Tracey?'

'Jack. Have I told you recently you are an idiot?'

'Can we change the record?'

'No, we can't, because literally no one else our age knows what a record is.'

This wasn't going well. He had hoped to talk to Tracey about what he'd discovered, she seemed to have a different agenda for the call. 'What's wrong?'

'Gavin and I have been talking.'

'Oh, yes? More wedding plans? I've agreed to go on his stag do, haven't I?'

'I don't think that's appropriate now. We've been talking. About that night out we had in Snobs a few months back? I had to head back to the hotel early because I was on my, you know?'

Jack had a sinking feeling that he knew where this was going.

'And I was worried about leaving you with Gavin and whether you would have much to talk about?'

He couldn't take the leading on anymore. 'What did he tell you, Tracey?'

'He told me.' Tracey was now shouting down the phone. 'He told me that you practically molested him as soon as I was out the door, that you grabbed his crotch and felt him up!'

'That did not happen, Tracey!' He tried to keep his voice calm. Exaggerated though the claim was, there was a tiny germ of truth in what she was saying. I bet Gavin didn't say, Jack thought, that he, in turn, had grabbed Jack's crotch and had released the top two buttons of his Levi's 501s. Their mouths had locked together for a good five minutes before Gavin had freaked out and pushed Jack away.

'Why would he say that if it wasn't true?' Tracey was becoming unintelligible, whether through anger or crying, it was hard for Jack to tell. 'I asked him why he'd been so funny when I mentioned your name recently. I thought you'd had a barney with him over the wedding. You do know I wanted you to give me away?'

'That's very kind of you. I'd be honoured.'

'That was before I found out you slept with my fiancée!'

'I didn't actually sleep-' Jack started, but Tracey spoke over his protestation.

'And when I think all the things I've told you about us, and you just wanted to get into his pants!'

There was no use in Jack saying anything. He just listened to the stream of vitriol and abuse that came from his best friend. He had screwed up, and he knew that there was a price to pay for that.

'I don't know if I can trust him - if I can trust you - anymore.'

Jack took a deep breath. One more lie was needed. 'Tracey, I'm sorry. It was all my fault. I led Gavin on, and he wouldn't have done anything if I hadn't approached him first. He's a good man. He was missing you, and I took advantage of the situation. I'm sorry.'

The line was silent apart from Tracey's heavy breathing and the occasional sniff. For nearly thirty seconds, there was nothing. Then she responded.

'Don't call me again, Jack.'

Three beeps indicated that she had terminated the call.

Feeling low after his conversation with Tracey, Jack didn't feel much like cooking that evening. A couple of beers later, he felt even less like preparing something healthy. A few taps on an app, though, and another pizza was ordered for delivery. He was going to have to do a lot of running to mitigate the junk food this week.

He tried to put the phone call behind him. He wasn't going to kiss and tell, but he wasn't the only one who had been at fault that evening. He and Tracey had had their fallings-out before, but this felt end-of-friendship serious. He tried to put himself in her shoes, but he just couldn't comprehend how she might be feeling.

He grabbed another bottle of gassy beer and glanced out of the apartment window in case the pizza was delivered early. There was a police car outside. This was surprising in itself. His area of town was normally free of trouble, one of the reasons he had selected this particular estate to live in. He didn't want trouble on his own front doorstep.

The intercom buzzer rang. The pizza delivery guy must have parked around the corner, he surmised. Not wasting any time, Jack barked, 'Top floor!' into the intercom and pressed the button to let them in.

A couple of minutes later, there was a knock at the front door. Jack already had the twenty-pound note in his hand for the transaction. He opened the door. Instead of a pepperoni and garlic bread, two police officers he didn't recognise were standing there. Only afterwards did he consider that they must have been brought in from another station to ensure that there was no unpleasantness in having to arrest their own colleague.

'Jack Appleyard?

'Yes?' He had that nauseous and sinking feeling in his stomach again, after so many years for Jack to be on the receiving end of this kind of interaction with the police.

'Can we step inside, please?' Both flashed their warrant cards. True enough, the photos of Sergeant Grace Baker and Constable Jason Wilson matched the people standing in front of him, as if anyone would be stupid enough to try and falsely pass themselves off as a police officer. He knew this wasn't a routine door-to-door inquiry, a sergeant doesn't come calling to reassure the public about local thefts or anti-social behaviour.

The usual pleasantries were exchanged, drinks offered and politely declined. They got him to confirm his date of birth and that he was indeed a suspended police officer. He, in turn, felt that it was appropriate to ask which division they worked for.

'Wednesbury, though the police station there is pretty well mothballed.' That would explain why didn't recognise the pair. His dealings with the town in the heart of the Black Country was limited to a few five-a-side friendlies and the occasional meeting on training courses. Jason seemed to spend all his time looking in his notebook and taking copious notes, even when Jack wasn't saying anything, which was a little disconcerting. It was a technique he'd have to remember when he was reinstated, he thought optimistically.

Grace was clearly in charge; a middle-aged, middle-career sergeant who had an agenda. If only Jack knew what that agenda was. Having had more time to examine her, he sensed he recognised her from somewhere - not directly work-related, but somewhere. It would be bad form, he knew, to reach for his phone and scroll through his photos. This train of thought distracted him momentarily from their conversation.

'Did you hear me, Mr Appleyard?' asked PC Wilson.

'I'm sorry?'

'I asked if you were aware of why we were here?'

He knew from being on the opposite side of

this conversation too many times that there were two main ways he could respond. He could be honest and effectively convict himself even before he was arrested, or he could plead ignorance. Luckily for Jack, he had a face which could, when required, exuded dumb innocence.

'I'm really sorry, but no, I haven't a clue. Is it something to do with my suspension?'

'No, Mr Appleyard.' The constant repetition of 'Mister' was clearly meant to put Jack in his place in the pecking order. 'We are investigating at least two incidents, of which we are aware, of you impersonating a police officer, and another one implicating you in the theft of personal property, specifically the mobile phones of a Mr Nick Whitehouse and Ms Julie Barr.'

'I have no idea who they are.'

'They are the parents of Martin Barr, the unfortunate young man who died at Chasewater last Sunday, and with whom we know you had, ahem, interactions on the dating app Grindr.' Grace wasn't referring to any notes; she knew the details well enough by heart.

So, the game was up, but that didn't necessarily mean that he had to go down quietly. Also, there was something Jack had to deal with before he left the apartment, especially if they sought a warrant to search the place. He would have to try and do something about that. He could hardly argue that he and Martin weren't connected, however.

'I didn't realise that it was an offence to know someone who had been murdered?'

'That's not what we are here for.' A note of tetchiness in her voice, Grace was starting to lose her cool. 'We would like you to come down to the station with us and answer a few questions if you would be so kind.'

'Am I under arrest?'

'Not yet no. Believe it or not, West Midlands Police doesn't like taking police officers, even ones under suspension, into police stations with handcuffs on or even locking them in cells. Can we just say that you are 'helping police with their inquiries'?'

Jack considered resisting, calling his police federation representative, and not going with the two officers to whichever police station they would take him to. Surely, they wouldn't humiliate him further and take him into Brownhills station itself for questioning? But he also realised that the only advantage would be to annoy two fellow officers who, so far, had been respectful and polite. 'That's fine, but just two points. Firstly, can I put something more than my lounge shorts and vest on?'

'No problem at all, though I would ask that Jason accompany you to ensure that you don't, ah, tamper with any evidence that there may be. And the second?'

'I have a pizza delivery due any minute. Can we wait for that to arrive?'

Jack needed to provide a necessary diversion. Not for one minute did he think that Jason had anything but a professional interest in him, but he needed to distract him for a short while.

He headed into the bedroom, closely followed by Jason. He could hardly give much of a striptease while only wearing two items of clothing, so he shucked them off quickly and threw them into the laundry basket in the corner of the bedroom. He then took his time looking in his built-in wardrobe, deciding what to wear, hands on hips, legs slightly apart, providing the copper with a perfect view of his rear. Jack imagined the discomfort that Constable Wilson would be in. He looked over his shoulder and as expected Jason was looking out of the window, staring at the ceiling, looking anywhere except directly at Jack's arse. Suitably distracted, Jack picked a jacket from his wardrobe, apparently at random, and palmed the two mobile phones which he had hidden in the inside pocket only a few hours before.

'Ah, there they are!' Jack exclaimed and squatted down to ostensibly pick a pair of trainers. He also placed the mobile phones deep inside one of the twenty-plus shoe boxes that he had stacked at the rear of the wardrobe. It still wasn't ideal, but it was the best he could do in the limited circumstances. Even if Jason had been looking in his direction, he was unlikely to have seen anything untoward. As it was, Jack noted that Jason was surreptitiously looking in the top drawer of one of Jack's bedside cabinets. Expecting something titillating, he looked disappointed to find only back issues of Private Eye.

'You'll find the second drawer down is more interesting,' Jack said cheekily. Jason, if it was possible, blushed a deeper red.

With the mission accomplished, Jack finally dressed in boxers, jeans, and a polo shirt for the police station. Remembering that, even in summer, the cells could be cool, he also grabbed a hoodie from the chest of drawers. Although he was fully clothed, Jason still seemed to be a little uncomfortable in Jack's presence as they headed back into the lounge.

Just as they were about to leave, the pizza finally arrived. There was a brief debate about what to do with the takeaway order but given that there were three police officers present in the room, the discussion wasn't that protracted. The pizza, along with Jack, went with them in the patrol car.

The journey back to Wednesbury Police Station was long enough for them to consume the pizza between them, and they had a pizza to consume before they got there, but that didn't stop Jack feeling that the questioning started as soon as they got in the car. This was completely at odds with official police guidelines. In 'blue light' reality programmes, officers seemed to spend all their time talking to dashboard cameras and analysing in front of suspects exactly what crime they think had been committed. In reality, most journeys were conducted in sullen silence.

'How have you found life since you've, ah, had more time to yourself? Found things to keep yourself occupied?'

'Well, you know how it is.' Jack was careful about what he said to Grace. Jason seemed engrossed in driving, though not averse to taking the occasional slice of pepperoni pizza when offered to him.

'We missed you at the Pride parade this year.'

Ah, that was where he had met Grace before. Each year since 2015, West Midlands Police had a presence in the main parade at Birmingham Pride. Whilst it was usual for police officers to march in their uniforms, these were usually adorned with lanyards in the pride colours, and Hawaiian Leis made of bright colours.

'I'm sorry, Grace, I didn't recognise you out of context. How's your partner - Susie, isn't it?'

'Sharon, and she's not my partner now.'

'I'm sorry to hear that.'

'She's my wife. She finally made an honest woman out of me.'

Despite the surreal situation, Jack was genuinely pleased for Grace and now remembered that the two had marched hand-in-hand at Pride.

Given the situation, it was nice to have a slightly friendlier face in the car.

'Jason here was my maid of honour, what with my family being Jehovah's Witnesses.' Jason practically tugged his forelock, which Jack caught in the rear-view mirror. Something told him that Jason hadn't had much choice in the matter.

'Congratulations, both of you. Maybe when all this is over we can have a proper catch-up.'

'Maybe, but it may not be over for a long time for you. Here we are.'

They pulled into the station and parked next to a couple of other police cars at the rear of the stark, utilitarian building. It had been constructed in the seventies when local policing was much more prevalent. The town had done well to keep the station open in the face of swinging cuts over recent years.

The custody sergeant was officious but friendly enough. It helped that it was still early on Friday evening. It would get very busy in the cells later on. Jack's pockets were emptied, including his mobile phone, and he was escorted to a cell.

'Is there anyone you want us to call?' So far everyone had been unfailingly polite.

'Just the duty solicitor, if you can, Simon.' Always good to remind the custody sergeant that you'd been to the party to celebrate his thirty years in the force.

The sergeant had the decency to look

sheepish. 'No problem, Jack. Let's get this sorted.'

Jack settled into the cell, which had been refurbished and was cosy in its own way. But it was still a custody cell in the police station in which, until four months ago, he had been a police constable.

Knowing that he could be in for a long wait, he settled back on the rubber mattress, which smelt slightly of Dettol. It could be worse, although he had already decided that there was no way he was ever going to use the seatless aluminium toilet in the corner, especially with the CCTV camera in the opposite corner of the cell. Jack closed his eyes and tried to relax.

Despite the stressful situation, he drifted. Not exactly to sleep, but to a place where he could at least zone out the persistent noise of the air circulation system, and the odd shout as other arrested miscreants were shown to their room for the night.

His legal representative arrived a few hours later, just after eleven o'clock, and they were allowed into one of the interview rooms unescorted. Jack had been given a bottle of water as a courtesy, and he sipped at it and looked over at his 'brief'. Jack guessed her age at mid-twenties. She was wearing blue jeans and a pale blue top and appeared breathless even though the walk from the front of the station to the cells was hardly strenuous.

'My name is Ann Jones, I'm your legal representative. I'm sorry it's taken me so long, it's been quite a night. '

'Tell me about it, Ann.'

'I'm a legal executive with Johnson, Johnson and Johnson.'

Jack suppressed a laugh. He thought that most solicitors had merged to form larger partnerships. The duty rota which had landed him with Ann clearly hadn't worked in his favour.

He was still processing the company name when something else hit him. 'A legal executive?' In the legal pecking order, a Legal Executive was one below a solicitor or one above a paralegal.

'I can assure you that I'm fully conversant with the incidents that may have brought you into this situation, Mr Appleyard.'

'Call me Jack.'

'Thanks, Jack. I have some good news for you already.' Despite his misgivings, Jack's heart leapt a little at hearing this. 'I'm pleased to say that they will not be raising any charges of impersonating a police officer.'

'Really?'

'Yes. I understand that whilst suspended from the force, you are still a serving police constable, even if you're not on active duty. Whether you choose to wear a uniform or not when you go for your daily walk is not technically illegal. It may not be sensible, but that doesn't seem to have been an issue for you over the last few days. Does it, Jack?' Ann's demeanour had changed radically over the few minutes of the conversation. She had very quickly grasped an argument for dropping the most worrying charge against him, and he was willing to comply.

'Er, yes, absolutely. And if I happened to get waylaid and enter someone's property dressed in said uniform?'

'A bathroom emergency. You got caught short when out on your daily walk and had no option but to ask to use someone's bathroom. It was mere misfortune on your part that this happened to be the local Morrissons supermarket, and the home of a recently deceased person who I understand was already known to you. It was that, or you would have been charged with indecent exposure. Ha.' Her laugh was humourless.

'Ha,' Jack replied in the same humourless tone.

'The other charges - the theft of the mobile phones - are causing some concern. There's likely to be CCTV of any alleged incident, as I understand these both may have happened in public areas?'

'Ah, yes.' Jack, in theory, was unable to say where the phones had been stolen. This was like playing chess, he thought.

'So, I suggest therefore when Sergeant Baker interviews you in around fifteen minutes, that you emphasise this point. Answer 'no comment' to any awkward questions or wait for me to answer on your behalf and agree to be bailed until such evidence is provided to the police. Then the Crown Prosecution Service can make an appropriate case for you.'

From suspecting that he was about to be brought in front of a court and possibly placed on remand, he couldn't believe that this Legal Executive, through a very loose interpretation of the law and insisting that evidence be gathered from not one but two separate CCTV systems, had managed to get him bailed.

'Ann, I'd like to thank you for all your help.'

'It's my job.' She started gathering her paperwork together to await Grace's arrival.

'How much of this did Sergeant Baker suggest to you?'

Ann stopped filling her briefcase and gave Jack a curious look. 'I think you've spent too long in the cells, Jack. You've got completely the wrong idea. Grace and I have not discussed your case at all in the canteen before coming to see you, and I would suggest that it would be advisable to remember that.'

Jack gulped. He couldn't make eye contact with the young woman. 'Yes, ma'am.'

CHAPTER NINE

Jack returned home via taxi in the early hours of Saturday morning. He had hoped he would be given a lift back in a police car but given that this was the busiest time of the week for officers across all but the most rural of stations, he was simply glad he had been processed and been left to his own devices to make his way home. Despite the stress of the previous day, he was exhausted and, once home, fell into a deep sleep.

All had worked out as Ann had predicted. He was bailed pending the securing of the CCTV footage from the two premises, or the discovery of the mobile phones. Warrants were not easily obtained over a weekend. A judge would have to decide that there was an urgent and pressing need for one, and that could not be demonstrated by Grace and her team. Jack hoped that by Monday, all of this would be over.

Jack still saw Saturday as the start of the weekend, even though as a copper he'd rarely had time off on Saturday or Sunday. He liked going to the gym early on a Saturday morning. It was quiet, and before the children crowded out the swimming pool, there was usually a lane free for him to swim by himself. Even today, later than usual, it was quiet. A leisurely sixty-four lengths would be a mile, split into groups of eight or ten with a breather in-between. He wasn't going for a specific time, but he felt the exercise would help undo much of the junk food he had consumed during the week.

This week had been exceptional for Jack, and he had much to think about as he swam, with only half an eye open through his dark goggles to make sure he wouldn't bump into anyone. His smartwatch counted the laps for him, so he would know when he had completed his round.

His watch vibrated to show that he had completed the mile-long swim and he moved out of the lanes to wallow in the shallow end of the pool. More out of habit than any real interest, he had a perfunctory look at the other men in the pool. There was the usual assortment of dad bods around, with children wearing armbands or throwing plastic toys around in the junior pool. There were a couple of swimmers using the lanes as earnestly as Jack had been, but they swam by so fast it was hard to make out any detail beyond a vague impression of sleekness.

Jack wondered if Martin had been a good swimmer, and then realised it wouldn't have made any difference. Tracey had told him that there was no water in his lungs - correction, lung - so he had been killed or knocked unconscious before being left in the water to die. This thought made him feel even more morose. He resolved to get out of the water and make the best of the rest of the day.

He used the communal changing rooms, then settled in at the café for a coffee and catch-up on his phone. His Twitter feed was full of the hashtag #sousvide, and some incident at the garden centre. But beyond this he had no idea what this related to, and the postings weren't giving much away. He continued to read the postings. They were all from local people that he followed. Jack knew some of them were anonymous accounts from his former colleagues who didn't want to follow the rigid social media guidelines meted out by their superiors, so hid under pseudonyms and even pretended to work in other areas of the country to avoid detection.

Had he not been a complete idiot and let his lower brain lead him astray in a nightclub several months ago, he may have been able to contact Tracey and find out what was happening, but as things stood, he knew any query to her wouldn't be welcome. He wasn't yet ready to apologise further; Gavin needed to do his bit, too. The WhatsApp message Jack had received overnight from Gavin, whilst his phone was in a secure locker under the watchful gaze of the custody officer, seemed to indicate that wouldn't be happening any time soon.

He only had one contact left who would be able to help him out and confirm what had happened. He drank as much of the scorching hot coffee as he could and headed to his car. This wasn't a conversation he could have in a public place.

'Alan, it's Jack.'

'Oh, hi, are you OK?'

Alan sounded nervous, and Jack could understand why. There was a standing rule that serving police officers shouldn't talk to recently suspended and arrested coppers who were out on bail on a technicality, especially on phones which could be traced to both of them. Even Alan, for whom the term 'plod' had been invented, knew that it wasn't a good idea.

'I just need some help. I've been looking on Twitter. Has something happened at a garden centre nearby?'

'Listen, mate, I'd love to help, but I can't.' There was a long sigh, and Jack waited. He knew that Alan would decide that the quickest way to get rid of Jack was to tell him what he wanted to know. 'I can't tell you that a body has been found in a hot tub at Grangemouth Garden Centre under suspicious circumstances.'

'Who is it?'

'We haven't got confirmation yet, but it's a young lad, late teens.'

'Are you there now?'

'I'm due to be on duty up there later, no doubt holding back the public. Again.'

'Alan, if I bought you a bottle of the best

rum I can find, would you be able to let me in?'

'No, Jack, absolutely not. I'm hanging up now. Goodbye'

It was good to know that there were still some coppers with morals, Jack thought. He had a very bad feeling. This was the same garden centre that Jack had visited the previous day to talk to Julie Barr. He remembered the vitriolic outburst that Martin's mother had unleashed when Fish's name had been mentioned, and Fish would certainly fit the description that Alan had provided.

He loaded Grindr on his phone and looked up Fish's profile. He hadn't been online for more than twenty-four hours.

Jack dropped him a message on WhatsApp, keeping it casual whilst also noting that his 'last seen' was also yesterday afternoon.

[Just checking in. Did you get back OK on Thursday?]

He got the single tick to show that it had been sent, but not the second tick to show it had been delivered. That meant that Fish's phone was off, out of range, or as Jack increasingly feared, waterlogged.

The garden centre was closed to the public, naturally. He drove past and police tape covered the front gate. A bored PCSO that Jack didn't know, maybe a new starter, waved on any traffic that tried to pull into the car park.

Jack drove on, parked in a country lane a few hundred yards away, and took a leisurely stroll through the fields and public footpath which ran along the back of the garden centre. He hopped over a small stile.

He couldn't risk dressing in uniform again. But maybe, just maybe, this would work. Although anyone passing by might think that he was a little overdressed for a Saturday morning walk, in a white short-sleeved shirt and tie, and a pair of casual chinos, with black patent leather shoes.

Unseen, he slipped into the disabled toilets at the rear of the garden centre using the staff entrance that the management had shared with him during his time as a copper. He knew the layout well. The centre had been a regular Sunday morning visit throughout his childhood for him and his parents until he had hit his sullen teenage years and stubbornly refused to go with them any longer. Later, as a police officer, he had found the free car parking and toilet facilities a boon when caught short during his shift, and the garden centre management were only too happy to have a police car and six-foot-two-inch copper strolling around.

He upended his Tesco carrier bag onto the toilet seat and unwrapped the contents. After some struggling in the limited space, he emerged from the toilets dressed head-to-toe in a white crime scene suit. The suit was actually a protective decorating coverall purchased from

B & Q en-route to the garden centre but would pass all but the closest of examination. With a dust facemask on from the same store and smart clothing underneath, he had an effective disguise, he hoped.

He strode confidently out of the centre itself and towards the hot tub franchise at the rear of the building. Half a dozen Jacuzzis in various sizes were scattered around. He was in luck, not recognising any of the CSI team. For the first time ever, he thanked the privatisation of forensic services.

He approached the person who seemed to be directing operations. They were focused upon a single large hot tub, the cover half-open. A forensics photographer was taking pictures with a giant SLR camera, fitted with a circular flashgun that distracted everyone with each shot.

'Can you tell me exactly what you've found?' Jack's voice was muffled slightly by the face mask. Maybe that would help disguise the nervousness in his voice.

'It's a male, late teens. Been in the water a good few hours, by the looks of it. The water temperature had been raised to over forty degrees, meaning that the body was lightly poached. Are you here to help retrieve the body?' Her voice was matter of fact, direct; maybe this was a frequent occurrence, and this was the third suspicious death in a hot tub she had dealt with this week, though Jack doubted it.

He gulped. Whilst his first few months as a police officer had eliminated any squeamishness in the job day-to-day, there were still situations that caused him to gag. Only last year, he had broken into the bungalow of an old lady who had died and been left alone for a couple of weeks with just her increasingly hungry cats for company. But this was the only way that he was going to get to see the body and confirm his worst fears.

He stepped forward. He could see the legs of the body, wrapped in cheap black polyester trousers. The shoes were also black, industrial style. As the rest of the body came into view, he saw a plain white t-shirt, such as that worn under a coverall, followed by a face that Jack recognised, despite its florid complexion and bloated features.

Jack's worst fears were confirmed. The face may not have been recognisable to anyone who hadn't spent time with Fish, but it was only two days since he had sat opposite this visage. It was now scarlet, the skin scalded by long immersion in hot water. There was no doubt in Jack's mind that Fish had been conscious when he slipped or was pushed into the hot tub. The cover had then been lowered, locked, and Fish had drowned.

He wasn't the only person visibly upset by the retrieval of the body. Whilst it was difficult to judge the emotional responses of people dressed head-to-toe in white suits and face masks, the way that some were turning away, and others raised their hands to their mouths, showed that this was distressing for them.

As was expected of him, he reached forward as two others grabbed Fish's legs and supported his back, and Jack held the head. Through the latex gloves, Jack had expected the body to feel cold, as a body should, but latent heat from exposure to the hot tub had pumped heat into the corpse. As he was gently laid into the open body bag, the three people who had retrieved the body stood for a short while in respectful silence. This wasn't normal Jack knew, but the unusual manner of this death had affected everyone.

Jack had pushed his luck so far already today, but as the bag was zipped up, a thought crossed his mind. He headed back to the CSI officer.

'Yes?'

'Can I ask a question, ma'am?' When in doubt, obsequiousness sometimes worked as well as flirtation. Jack couldn't flirt with this woman, or any woman, really.

She looked up from her iPad expectantly.

'There was an air gap between the water and the cover. Surely, he couldn't have drowned if he had air?'

'You wouldn't have thought so,' she replied, 'but the seal between the cover and the hot tub is airtight to help with insulation. The air would have got stale within about five minutes as CO_2 levels increased.'

'Could he not have lifted the cover?'

'It had a child safety lock on the outside, to

prevent this type of accident happening in the first place. There was no way it could be opened from the inside.'

'Can you tell the SIO that the victim's name is Billy Preston. He's a known associate of Martin Barr, who was killed last Sunday at Chasewater. The two deaths have to be linked.'

'And who exactly are you?' Against all protocols, the CSI officer reached up to remove Jack's facemask. If Jack had been thinking straight, he would have exclaimed something dramatic like, 'A friend!' But with this being real life, Jack could only mumble an apology and quickly walk away. Luckily the back entrance across the stile was still unguarded, and it was the work of a moment to tear off the bunny suit, face mask, and latex gloves. He could walk back to his car, still sweating profusely, but apparently undetected.

As Jack started the engine and let the air conditioning sweep over him, he had an idea. He grabbed his phone and texted Alan.

[What did the CCTV show?]

It took a few minutes for the reply to come through. He was probably working hard, maybe staffing the police cordon at the front of the garden centre.

[The cameras haven't worked for over a week. A pretty cheap system and didn't cover the back of the centre anyhow.]

[K, thanks]

Jack was sure that the official investigation

would have checked, but it intrigued him how the attacker knew that the CCTV was out of action. Surely, this pointed to an inside job, someone who knew they wouldn't be detected.

He drove back past the cordon, and sure enough, Alan had replaced the PCSO who had been on duty earlier. As he passed, Jack made eye contact and raised his hand in acknowledgement to Alan, who put his finger to his lips, making it clear that he expected Jack to keep the information he'd provided to himself.

Still trying to process what had happened to Fish, Jack found himself on autopilot heading to Chasewater. He stopped at the top of the park, near the heritage railway. He was a little surprised to find that the station was open, and they were running a normal service. He expected it to be closed for a while yet.

He flashed a smile at the lady at the ticket office, and whilst not being specific about why he wanted to speak to them, asked in a casual way whether the engine drivers who had seen the tragedy last week were available.

'You mean Tom and George? Yeah, they're in today, just getting the diesel ready for the next run. If you catch them quick, you'll find them in the engine. They'll be off in a bit, though.'

Jack hurriedly purchased a ticket and climbed aboard. He knew the timetable and that he would have more time to carry out his interview at the end of the short run.

The train headed off at a leisurely pace, and he wasn't surprised to find that he had most of the carriage to himself. The novelty of the long, hot summer had long since faded, and many potential visitors would probably have been put off by the recent events. There were a morbid few in the old mark II coach, gawking out the window. But they fell silent as the train went past Jeffrey's Swag and they saw the floral tributes to Martin by the side of the track. Jack sat there, his own eyes drawn to the bunches of flowers, lost in his own thoughts.

Just twenty minutes after setting out, the train pulled into the terminus at Burntwood Station, close to the home of Martin's parents. Indeed, the roof of their small home could be seen from the station platform. Jack alighted, and after making sure that he was the only one left on the platform, he made his way to the diesel shunter at the head of the train.

He approached the younger guy first, with an evens chance of getting the name correct.

'Excuse me, George? I was a friend of the guy who got killed last Sunday.' He held out his hand in greeting. George, in turn, held up his dirty hands to show why he couldn't shake hands. Though he hadn't been shovelling coal, the engine cab was still a dirty place.

'Oh, yes.' Followed by an awkward pause. 'It's Tom you'll want to be talking to.' The response wasn't the friendliest, but at least he had acknowledged him. Jack guesses he was fed up answering questions, both the police and inquisitive volunteers.

'Who's after me?' Tom appeared from the front of the engine, where he had been checking some pressure gauge, no doubt.

'I was just explaining to George here,' Jack said, bringing the youngster into the conversation as if they were lifelong buddies, 'that it seemed a bit quick to be reopening the railway.'

George looked down and wiped his hands with an oily rag like it was the most important thing in the world to him.

'Well, yes, but this is the peak season for us. Apart from the Santa and Halloween specials, of course. We're a charity. No trains, no income. Ain't that right, George?'

At a loss to add to the conversation, George just nodded. 'You don't feel it's right, though, do you, Tom? You said it was too soon.'

Tom drew in a breath, as if he was about to declare something profound. But instead, all that he said was, 'That it is, lad, that it is.'

Feeling that he was intruding on their grief, he couldn't go without checking something. Feeling like Columbo, he asked, 'One last question: did either of you know Martin? I'm guessing you've seen his picture in the papers?'

Tom shook his head, but the younger one nodded. 'I've seen him on the station a few times we've come in, with his tripod set up over there.'

He pointed towards the end of the platform. 'He preferred the steam engines. They're more... what's the word? Photowotsit.'

'Photogenic?'

'That's the bugger. But he took a mean picture of the trains. He showed me a couple of them on his camera. He had a mate with him once, young lad, about my age.'

Jack found his eyes brimming with tears, still unable to connect the bright, vibrant lad that he'd met with the bloated corpse he'd seen less than an hour ago. 'That would have been his friend, Billy. We just had some bad news about him, too, I'm afraid. It appears he has also died in suspicious circumstances.'

George visibly sagged. Tom took his peaked cap off and held it in front of him. 'There's something seriously wrong with this place if two lads like that can end up dead in a week.' George was also filling up with tears. 'They seemed like great lads. I know what they're saying in the paper about Martin being gay and all, but he was still a good laugh.'

Instinctively, Jack reached in and rubbed George's shoulder in a friendly manner. This was the only person he had met all week who'd had any sort of emotional response to what now must be considered a double murder.

'I'd, ah, better get on.' Jack stumbled. 'Thanks to you both for your help.'

George composed himself, wiping snot

away on his boiler suit arm, as Tom busied himself with preparing the diesel engine for the return journey.

Jack decided he'd had enough of the train for one day and walked across the grassland back to the station. This inevitably meant that he came again across the memorial to Martin. The intense heat of the last few days had caused many of the floral tributes to dehydrate and wither quickly. Jack wondered whether they would still be there in a week's time, or if they would be nibbled away by the deer that roamed freely on Chasewater.

Jack flopped down on his leather sofa, can of beer in hand, and started flicking through the channels to try and find something to watch. He was just wondering whether to fire up the laptop to find something to pass the time. He'd barely reached over before his phone pinged. How old-fashioned, was his first thought a text message. And from an unknown number.

His first suspicion was that it was a former one-night stand getting in touch, but he was meticulous in recording numbers of people he had 'encountered' just in case.

[This is Amanda, Phil's fiancée. I need to talk to you.]

Jack stared at the screen. Why would she want to contact him now? It had been four months since the terrible incident, and whilst he was still incredibly remorseful about what had happened to

Phil, he couldn't think what Amanda could need to talk to him about.

He couldn't ignore the text though and wondered how she had got hold of his number. Perhaps through Tracey. Maybe she had been holding on to the request from Amanda for a while and had only now shared his number in some sort of spiteful revenge. He had to respond, and he knew he had to meet her, but she certainly wasn't coming to his home. It wouldn't be good to be in private with her, he knew that much. And there was no point in putting off the inevitable.

[Do you know the BJ Diner on the A5? See you there at 4 p.m.]

[That's fine, see you there/then.]

The diner had been a mistake, he realised that now. Whilst the air conditioning was a welcome relief from the oppressive heat, it was still busy with families, driven to distraction at this point in the school holidays and desperate for something for the children to do. It was the third time in the week that Jack had been there and was greeted as a familiar face by the surly waitresses. Almost.

Amanda came in a few minutes later and slipped into the red padded seat opposite Jack. The last time he had seen her was at the hospital during Phil's recovery. She had just come from work and had been dressed in a smart tweed trouser suit and a white blouse. Today she wore jeggings, a loose t-shirt and hardly any make-up. The difference couldn't have been more radical, and Jack wondered yet again for the hundredth time since the message had appeared why she wanted to meet him.

'Amanda?' He didn't mean it to be a question; he was still taken aback. She must have noticed his shocked look.

'Don't look at me like I'm something the cat dragged in,' she snapped back immediately, 'It's not exactly been a fun few months for me.'

'I'm sorry, your call came as a surprise.'

The waitress, who had been hovering since Amanda had sat down, appeared at their elbows yet again. They ordered coffees and waited for her to move out of earshot before continuing.

'This isn't my idea of a fun afternoon, I can assure you. You haven't even asked how Phil is.'

'I'm sorry.' How many times had he said that over the last few months? He should set it as a standard text reply on his phone. 'I hear that the rehab work has been good for Phil.'

'Well, yes. He's still not walking, but he does have good upper body strength. There's an outside chance that he may regain the use of his legs, but it's not certain.'

'I should go and see him when the disciplinary has been sorted.'

'That's what I want to talk to you about. Phil has been asked to provide a statement to the tribunal.'

Suddenly, the call made sense to Jack. He tried to keep his voice as neutral as possible. 'Oh, yes? What is Phil going to say?'

'There are three options, Jack. First option is the truth: that he remembers nothing from the moment he got you that bloody coffee from McDonalds. Do you realise how often I've had to hear about the woman in there offering him the drink for free? It's the last thing he remembers before waking up in the hospital. He's obsessed with her.'

'You said three options.' Jack didn't like where he thought this was heading.

'The second option is that Phil decides that he can remember more - that you did the best to protect him, and that as far as he's concerned no blame can be attached to you for what was a tragic accident. Maybe even that Phil was stupid to try and tackle the thief on his own.'

'Well, that's near enough the truth. But why would Phil lie if he can't remember anything?'

'Because you're going to give us ten grand. That would make a big difference to us here and now. The compensation from the Police will take years to come through. We need to make adaptions to the house now. We're spent up.'

Jack sat in silence for a while. He had the cash, although it would wipe out his life savings and he would have to put off his new car for another year or so. But there was no doubt that Phil admitting that he had made mistakes that night would go a long way to getting him off the hook and maybe back onto the force. But...

'You mentioned a third option.'

Amanda took a careful sip of her coffee and placed the cup down before speaking again. Her voice changed to a hoarse whisper. 'The third option. I... I mean, Phil says that he remembers being concerned about going into the garden on his own, but you overruled him and ordered him into the situation, fully aware of the dangers. Maybe you'd even said that you had seen something glinting at head-height and admitted that you were scared, too, but insisted that Phil went in first.'

'That's not true!' Jack exclaimed, louder than he intended, drawing the attention of other diners.

'It doesn't really matter, does it?' Amanda replied. 'If you want to be sure of the right outcome, you know what you need to do.' She slid a piece of paper over the table to him. All it had on it was an email address. 'Send the money via PayPal. That's all you need. Less traceable than a bank account transfer. You have one week - no need to contact me or Phil again.'

She stood, leaving her coffee untouched and walked out. There were no pleasantries. This was a simple blackmail. He knew what he should do: ring his Police Federation rep and explain exactly what had happened. But then again, if ten grand would get him back onto the Force, shouldn't he consider it? Jack balanced the three options up in his mind.

Despite all that had been going on, Jack had a prior commitment which he would not break. Once he got home, he showered again, changed into chinos and a smart short-sleeved shirt, and drove to Blake Street station to catch the train to Birmingham city centre.

The weekly concert at Symphony Hall was a guilty pleasure and one that he had told very few friends about. It interfered little with his social life, if he was out in town on a Saturday it would rarely be before ten o'clock anyhow that he would meet up.

It started when Jack was at school. He used to go to the youth orchestra concerts, then watched clips on YouTube of his favourite pieces of classical music. One of his first boyfriends was a percussionist in the Birmingham Gay Symphony Orchestra, and even though the relationship had lasted shorter than Wagner's Ring Cycle, he had resurrected an interest in classical music that wasn't 'cool', but the regular concert going brought some stability to Jack's occasionally unstructured life.

There was little point in booking a season of concerts. With Jack's shifts, he was never sure from one week to the next whether he would be free, but the concerts were very rarely filled to capacity.

He dodged the bikes riding through the newly renovated Centenary Square, having checked ticket availability on his phone whilst on the train. It was a programme of popular light classics, ideal for a summer's evening. He popped to the box office, smiled at the ticket seller, and got a perfect seat in the upper circle for a relatively low price.

Jack settled into the seat. He didn't need a programme, all the music was familiar to him. He turned his phone off and waited for the music to overwhelm him.

The first piece, Ravel's Bolero, was simply intoxicating. The full fifteen minutes of the piece, and the absolute concentration of the percussionist on the snare drum who had taken centre stage, took Jack away from all his troubles. He closed his eyes and let the rhythm of the music fill his mind. For Jack, this couldn't be done with any other sort of music. He tried to pick out the clarinet, which had started the piece, but had since been lost in the rest of the orchestra. The fact that he had no control over the volume, couldn't rewind, couldn't even prevent the whispering of the obnoxious person two rows away, didn't distract from his enjoyment of the piece.

The next piece was more sedate and longer. Beethoven's Pastoral Symphony. The City of Birmingham Symphony Orchestra were doing a fine job. Probably due to his familiarity with the piece, Jack found himself drifting, not into sleep but a daydream state. He tried to tie the threads of what he now thought of as 'his' investigation together.

Just then, he heard the vibration of a phone somewhere along his row. He was tolerant of this behaviour - well, more tolerant anyhow than some of the audience who were audibly sighing at this intrusion. He leaned forward slightly to see a man in his early thirties, tall and gangly and folded into the seat like a piece of human origami, fumbling with a phone. The man then reached into another pocket and retrieved a second phone. This second phone was clearly the culprit. Jack pondered on this. He struggled sometimes to remember to pick up his one phone, let alone two. Presumably one was a work phone, and the unfortunate concertgoer was on call.

As he thought about this, he realised that the final piece of his jigsaw had fallen into place and how the murder of Martin Barr had been executed. Anyone watching him from the audience might wonder why the handsome young man spent the rest of the evening smiling to himself, not just because he was enjoying the rest of the concert.

CHAPTER TEN

Jack once again had hardly slept. He believed he knew exactly what had happened to Martin, and suspected that he knew what had happened to Fish as well. But the evidence was not yet incontrovertible.

He got up and went for an early morning run before the heat got too much for him, then returned and showered. Just one more confrontation, one more meeting, and maybe, just maybe, he could sleep better that night. But first, he needed back-up. Jack made himself a second espresso and grabbed his phone. It wasn't every day that you accused someone of murder, and before that he needed to eat the biggest portion of humble pie ever served.

'Tracey?'

'I thought I told you I didn't want to hear from you again.'

'I need your help - really, I do!'

'Is this about Martin?'

'Yes, and about his friend, Fish.'

'The one who was boiled in the hot tub.'

'Actually, it was sous vide. The temperature

wouldn't have been... never mind. Tracey I am really, really sorry about what happened with Gavin. I would have never done anything to harm our friendship.'

'But you did, though, you snogged my fiancé!'

'At least you believe me when I say that we didn't do anything more. If I tell you I have been an absolute complete idiot, it was totally a one-off thing, and I promise it will never happen again.'

The pause from the end of the phone was so long Jack thought the call had dropped. The silence seemed to continue for an eternity, until finally Tracey spoke. 'It's not you I believe so much as Gavin. He's been so apologetic since he confessed. There's no way he would ever cheat on me again.'

'So, are we OK? I really need your help, Tracey.'

'Well...' She paused. 'I remembered after I first started seeing Gavin at the start of last year. I was on Helen's pre-hen night bash with a few of her friends - you know Helen?'

'Didn't she get divorced earlier this year?'

'Yes, and this is my story Jack. Well, you know the Katy Perry song 'I Kissed a Girl'? That song came on and... I did.'

'Did what?'

'Kissed a girl. My old school friend, Tanya.'

She had fed Jack the line; it would have been rude for him not to give the appropriate response. 'And did you like it?' he asked.

'It was different. But what I'm trying to say is that, as long as you promise it was a one-off incident...?'

'It was, honestly, Tracey.' He wondered how far to push it. 'And it's not like he was that good a kisser, anyhow!'

'I know. I've lost count of how many times I've told him that his tongue feels like a squid in my mouth.'

They both laughed, Jack mostly with relief. 'So, can you help me?'

'I'm working until three.'

'No, this *is* work. You'll need to be in uniform, and you'll need to be ready to call for back-up.' Jack explained what he wanted her to do, and they set a time. 'I'll text some more information over later, but thanks again.'

'Laters.' Tracey hung up. Jack exhaled a large breath and slumped back on the sofa. He was incredibly relieved that he appeared to have salvaged his friendship with Tracey, it was only when he hadn't had her both as a sounding board and also telling him that he was being an idiot (and worse) that he'd realised how much he was missing her.

There was little point in Jack pretending that he was a serving police officer. The game was up in that particular regard. He decided to dress smartly, however, for the upcoming encounter. Tan chinos, white shirt and a pale blue jacket hinted at an authority that Jack didn't actually represent. Certainly, for a Sunday morning, he felt a little overdressed, but if 'clothes make the man' according to Mark Twain, then Jack was going to take any advantage that he could today.

After sending a last text, he put his phone in voice recorder mode and hit the red button. He doubted that anything that was said would be admissible as evidence, but every little helps. As prepared as he was ever going to be, Jack knocked loudly on the door of Seven Royston Road.

Nick Whitehouse opened the door to his home wearing jogging bottoms and a t-shirt. Jack reeled slightly both at his unshaven visage and the body odour that emanated from Martin's stepfather. Surprisingly, Nick didn't immediately slam the door in his face, but walked back through the narrow hall and into the lounge, leaving Jack to follow and close the door behind him. The television was on as before, with the Sunday morning chat and cooking show that acted as moving wallpaper for so many homes.

Julie was sat on the sofa, legs tucked underneath her, knitting some black shapeless object. Jack was aware that, so far, none of the people in this ridiculous tableau had spoken. Taking the initiative, Jack grabbed the remote control, turning off the television. Julie and Nick's reaction was impassive, Nick stared down at the grubby carpet, and Julie's needles continued to click away.

'I think you both know why I'm here, don't you?' At last, a response. Julie put down her knitting and placed it in the bag by her side.

'We don't even know your real name,' Nick replied. It was true, he'd used a false identity last time he had been in their house.

'It's Jack. I was a good friend of Martin.'

'You mean you're one of his fag friends?'

Jack bridled. 'We had this discussion before. Don't use that sort of language with me or else.'

'Or else what?' Nick retorted, standing up and bunching his fists aggressively.

'Well, as a minimum, it's a homophobic hate crime. But I think that's going to be the least of your problems, don't you? Why don't you both sit down. I'll explain what I've discovered, and then we can see what happens from there.'

'What if I call the police right now? I've got the Family Liaison Officer's number somewhere, for all the use that they've been.' Julie stared at Jack as she spoke, trying to intimidate him. But this time he had the upper hand.

'And what would you use to do that, then? A phone? And which phone would that be, Nick? The one that you handed to the police, which you use to manage your gambling debts? But that handset's been stolen. Or would you use the one that you kept for yourself and used to arrange the murder of your stepson?' Jack reached into his jacket and showed the two phones he had stolen from Julie and Nick the previous Friday.

'I knew you had my phone, you bastard! What are you doing with it?' Nick replied angrily. He stared at the phones as if Jack had just done a conjuring trick. Julie clutched her knitting bag tightly, seemingly in shock at the events that were happening.

'Checking when you last booked an Uber,' was Jack's simple reply.

'So? It's not against the law to book a taxi, is it? You've got no right to have my phone.'

'It's not against the law, no. But it would be of interest to a murder investigation to know if you were at Chasewater on the Sunday evening when you claimed to be at home watching the football on television, with your wife as your alibi. And whilst I'm not currently an active police constable, I do still have contacts within Brownhills Police Station to whom I can present this information. Indeed, for all you know, I might have already done that. I'm sure they can get a lot more information from this phone than I did just reading your notifications screen. And maybe wonder why you handed over a fake phone to the police when asked.'

Nick paled and gazed downwards, unable to answer.

'But I still want to hear from you why you did it. Why did you kill your stepson and leave him to be decapitated by the powerboats?' Nick sighed.

'That... that was never the plan,' he replied in a dull monotone. 'I never wanted him to come to any more harm. But she...' He stopped.

'Who's "she", Nick? Do you mean your wife?' Jack was totally focused on Nick, but he spotted a slight shift of the body from Julie, still perched on the other end of the sofa, and turned towards her. 'Was it you, Julie? Did you tell Nick to find Martin at Chasewater and... do what? Injure him? That wouldn't have been enough, would it? Even in a hoody or mask, I'm sure Martin would have been able to recognise his own stepfather. No, you sent Nick out with one clear aim that afternoon: whilst you were at work with plenty of witnesses at the garden centre, Nick knocked him unconscious and pushed him into the water, in the path of the speedboats to make doubly sure. You arranged all of this, didn't you?'

Julie snapped, in contrast to Nick's pale face she was flushed, colour rising to her cheeks. 'I wasn't going to have that filthy faggot in the house anymore, after he'd been hanging around with people like you. Just like his father. He was a poofter, too, you know, though I didn't know that before I married him. Oh no, he hid that well enough until I was pregnant. I should have known Martin would turn out that way. The clues were there.' The outburst was full of vitriol, directed at both Jack and her dead son.

The situation had escalated quickly, and for a few moments Jack was at a loss, wondering what to do with the information that he'd suspected for a while, but only now had been revealed to him. He hoped that his phone had recorded the confession, but even if it hadn't, he hoped there would be enough information on the phone that he was still holding to convict Nick. There was not one shred of regret in either of their body language.

'But that wasn't enough, was it, Julie? There was someone other than me who had put the clues together. Poor Fish. He approached you, didn't he?'

Julie appeared distracted again, rummaging around in her knitting bag. 'He led my Martin astray. I was trying to get him set up with someone good, a girl who would have put him on the straight and narrow in every way. But no, that slut came along in his skinny jeans and tight t-shirt, taking him to God-knows-what sort of bars.'

'And Fish came to you earlier in the week, didn't he? Maybe not here - he would be scared to come here wouldn't he after the roasting you gave him last time. Maybe he came to the garden centre? On Friday?'

'He came to my work, where anyone could have noticed us together, me and that gay slut! As if I'd want to be spotted with him. There was no way I was going to be seen talking to him,' she repeated. 'I told him to get a drink from the café and wait. I would see him after work.'

'Why did he hang around? I wouldn't have, the way you've been speaking to me.'

'I told him that I had some personal things that Martin would have wanted him to have. I told him they were in my car, and I couldn't get them until the end of my shift.'

'You'd have a set of keys to lock up?'

'I waited until everyone had gone home. He got bored, I guess, and started looking around the garden centre.'

'You were happy to talk to him when no one could see you together, when you couldn't be seen talking to the - what's the word you used? "Poofter"?'

'We walked and talked. I said I was locking up and checking all the doors. He said that he had loved my son. Can you believe it? He actually stood in front of me and said that he had feelings for Martin! How could he do that? When he saw how I felt, well, I think then he realised that maybe I had done something terrible. I would never have let him and my son be together. Not over my dead body.'

'Or Martin's? Or Fish's?'

'It was too easy. One of the hot tub covers was still open. You saw Fish's body, what a skinny little runt he was. You probably lust after him the way my Martin did, you pervert!'

'What happened next, Julie?' It was becoming increasingly hard for Jack to keep his cool, but he had to if he was going to finally get to the truth.

'I pushed him into the hot tub. It was so easy; I just pushed him in. And as he flailed around, I reached over and slammed the cover down and snapped the childproof straps shut. I turned the heat up to maximum and put the jets on, so he'd find it harder to breathe.'

'And walked away?'

'And walked away. I couldn't go back and check on him, could I? I walked out and locked up. I knew the CCTV had been knackered for weeks.'

Even though Jack had suspected that this was what had happened to poor Fish. To hear Julie talk about it in such a cold and calculated way was proving harder than he thought it would be. He could feel tears pricking at his eyes, not just at the death of Fish, but at the manner that he must have drowned. He took a few deep breaths, trying to compose himself. There was still unfinished business. He turned to Nick.

'And Martin? What happened over at Chasewater, Nick?'

Nick wouldn't make eye contact, focusing still on the invisible spot on the carpet. 'I knew Martin would be walking back home after the last race. It was easy enough to get an Uber round to that side of Chasewater, the path I knew he would be walking. I grabbed a stone. It was big, bigger than my fist.'

'And then what happened? What did you do, Nick?'

'I came up behind him and hit him on the back of the head. Hard. He crumpled as soon as I hit him. He didn't feel anything, I'm sure. There was some blood but not as much as I had thought there would be.'

'You killed him with that first blow Nick, your stepson.' The words Jack said came out calmly, even though Jack was feeling anything but. 'But that wasn't enough, was it?'

'I wanted to make it look like an accident, like he'd stumbled and fallen into the water.'

'As well as stealing his camera equipment and trying to sell it to help with your gambling debts?'

This alone seemed to make Nick angrier than the other accusations that Jack had made.

'I'd asked him for a loan a few times. He was hardly paying anything to live here. I think he was saving it so that he could shack up with that queerboy Fish. I only needed a couple of grand, just to get myself even, and then I would have been OK. And I would have paid him back, eventually.' Nick sighed, almost in relief.

'Where is his stuff?'

'In my locker at work. I was going to sell it to a mate there, but he wasn't interested when he heard about Martin. "Too soon," he kept saying, "too bloody soon."'

'But you'd been using Martin for weeks before that, hadn't you. All your shoplifting at the supermarket. You'd told him to turn a blind eye, and that lost him his job, because of the higher losses when he was on shift, that was all due to you. You loused up his career as well as his personal life. And all because he wouldn't fit in with the mould that you and Julie had cast for him.'

'It wasn't all one way, you know,' Julie interrupted. 'He wasn't easy to live with. So moody, secretive.'

'Are you surprised? I didn't know him well, but I'm sure that Martin could have done much better than living here with you two.' Anger was creeping into his voice now, and he felt he was losing control of the situation. He turned towards the French windows at the back of the lounge and gazed out, tried to relax the tight knot in his muscles.

Jack exhaled. He had a confession from each of them, recorded on his phone, but what could he do with it now? He turned back towards Julie and Nick. 'You know I'm not a serving police officer. Your confession means nothing, not really.'

Jack noted that Julie once again gripped her knitting bag, looking for something. 'So what happens now, then?' Nick seemed genuinely confused. Jack reached into his inside pocket and retrieved his own phone.

'I guess I'll have to take this to the police. A recording of the last fifteen minutes' conversation. Maybe they'll find Martin's camera equipment in your locker. At the very least, they'll check out this other phone Nick, the one you didn't hand over to the police'.

The roar from Nick came from deep in the throat and was almost inhuman, as he leapt from the sofa and tried to grab the phone from Jack's hands. Much as Jack had taunted both of them over the previous twenty minutes, he hadn't really been expecting the confrontation to become physical, they were two middle-aged, sedentary gits as far as he was concerned. He dropped the phones, leaving both of his hands free to grab Nick by the shoulders and push him down to his knees. The gym sessions he had maintained throughout his suspension were worth it, and he easily dominated the older man physically. But concentrating on Nick, Jack lost his focus on the other person in the room.

Julie hadn't been sitting on the sofa idly watching the fight between the two men. As Nick went down, arms grappled to his sides, she leapt up and tried to grab Jack's phone. In her other hand were a pair of dressmaking scissors used to cut cloth, retrieved from her knitting bag. Otherwise occupied subduing Nick, Jack didn't see the sharp metal point penetrate his left thigh until it was too late.

It was the dampness of the blood that he felt first before any pain. But then the slow burn started, and he had to let go of Nick as the pain overwhelmed him. Looking down at his thigh, he saw a near-perfect circle of blood staining the tan chinos, and at the bullseye, still sticking out and quivering with each beat of his accelerated pulse, were the scissors.

There was silence, apart from three people's laboured breathing. Nick slumped to the floor, unable to comprehend what had happened. Julie moved first, picking up the phones from the floor, and fumbled the lock of the French windows. She ran through the doors into the afternoon sun, intent on escape through the rear garden.

Jack was unaware of much of this. The sight of blood, especially his own, made him feel faint. As the trouser leg became more blood-soaked, he slumped down onto the floor, unable to move. Through half-closed eyes he watched Julie's receding figure, unable to do anything but clutch his thigh.

Julie ran out of the house and into the garden. She had no plan in mind but to escape. The small garden was more of a yard with no flower beds or ornaments, grassed to the edges with a small shed in the far corner.

She headed for the back gate, stopping to open the bolt, and ignoring Nick's shouts behind her. She clumsily fumbled with the latch, struggling with the mobile phones still in her hands, and pulled it towards her.

There was a flash of black from the corner of her eye, before she was down on the floor. Tracey had been hiding behind the shed, and seeing her opportunity, had bowled Julie over. Straddling her with Julie's hands help behind her back, she called to Jack for support. Julie struggled underneath her, but Tracey's weight meant that she was unable to move.

'Jack, I need some help here!' Tracey called back into the house. She could hardly see inside - the contrast between the bright sunshine and the dark household interior was too much - but she could make out the outline of two people on the floor one slumped against the sofa at an unusual angle.

Reaching behind for her handcuffs, she had to improvise and secured Julie to a fencepost. It was hardly proper procedure, but that was the least of her problems. Calling for an ambulance into her Airwave, she went to Jack's side, pushing a stumbling and still-shocked Nick out of the way.

She straightened Jack out, so that he was flat on his back, still bleeding profusely from the thigh. The scissors were still in the wound, pulsing gently. She was afraid that the femoral artery had been hit, but removing the weapon could cause more damage, remembering her first aid training. Jack's eyes were open, but his breathing was shallow, and reedy. Classic signs of shock.

'You!' she shouted at Nick. 'Lift that leg above your shoulder. Put your hand here and press hard around the wound. Don't you fucking touch those scissors or I will brain you!' She pointed towards the centre of the stain on Jack's thigh. The French windows were still open, and she could hear Julie exhorting Nick to help her instead of 'that police bitch'. Nick knelt by Jack and followed the PCSO's orders. Tracey noted that the blood flow appeared to have stopped.

'Thanks Tracey,' was all that Jack could manage.

'What a fucking mess.' Was all that Julie could manage in response.

'Phones... get the phones.'

Over her own heavy breathing, Nick's quiet whimpering, and Julie's shouted obscenities from the end of the garden, it was hardly surprising that Tracey didn't hear the sirens of the police cars and ambulance until they were nearly at the door.

When they stormed in, there were suddenly far too many people in the room. She left Jack to the professionals. Three paramedics came in dressed in green. Tracey was pleased to see that it was PC Alan Coleman who had responded to her call. They both took Nick outside to the relative peace of the back garden.

'Nick Whitehouse, I am arresting you on suspicion of the murder of Martin Barr. You do not have to say anything, but it may harm your defence if you do not mention, when questioned, something which you later rely on in court.' She continued to caution him, whilst Alan handcuffed his hands securely behind his back. She placed both Nick's second phone, and Julie's phone that she'd sent messages to Fish on into evidence bags.

The paramedics had taken over the house, so it was easiest to take Nick out through the back gate. Julie was still handcuffed to the fence post. With her free hand, she lashed out at him as he was walked past, scratching his face. 'You stupid idiot!' she screamed. 'It's all your fault!'

Head down, he didn't respond to her taunts.

Tracey turned to Julie, making sure that she was out of reach of her manicured nails. Another police officer restrained her and ensured that she could cause no more injury. 'Julie Barr, I am arresting you on suspicion of the murder of William Bishop, and the attempted murder of Jack Appleyard.' She thought about it for a moment. 'And assault against Nick Whitehouse.' She was hoping the CPS would also consider the issue of homophobic hate crime. But she had other matters to deal with and the charge sheet could always be tidied up back at the station by the custody officer.

Tracey returned to the lounge, where Jack was being placed on a stretcher. His eyes were still open, but the faraway look told Tracey he was under the influence of morphine. He gave the weakest of thumbs-up, which Tracey returned, before he was taken through the front door by the paramedics.

CHAPTER ELEVEN

The day of the tribunal, after nearly five months of anticipation, was something of an anticlimax. So many reports had been prepared on both sides, that Jack was sure the panel had already made up their mind about his future career in the force.

The room in which the tribunal was held was windowless, a low ceiling adding to the feeling of claustrophobia for everyone, and the air conditioning was running on maximum. Everyone was in their most formal uniforms, with the exception of Jack Appleyard, who wore a dark blue double-breasted suit jacket, bought the day before from Next, with Tracey's help. At least he could reuse it for the wedding next year.

His Police Federation representative made an impassioned defence, explaining how Jack had been a valued and experienced Police Constable. Whilst his homosexuality wasn't explicitly stated, his advocate made reference to Jack being a 'pioneer for his community' and an exemplar of what an officer of West Midlands Police should strive to be.

The tragic incident that had led to the inquiry was an unfortunate set of circumstances that could not have been anticipated, he said. Any error in judgment came not from PC Appleyard, but rather Special Constable Philip Parker, who was inexperienced and unable to adapt to a rapidly changing situation in which he found himself. Motioning to the former Special Constable who sat in his wheelchair alongside his girlfriend, the representative continued with his argument. He noted that whilst he and Jack Appleyard continued to wish Philip a continued improvement in his recovery, the sequence of events which led to the injuries sustained is unfortunately as much his responsibility as that of the accused officer.

Jack couldn't even look at Phil. It was the first time he had seen him in six months. His fiancée Amanda, was dressed much more modestly than the last time they had met at the BJ Diner, now wearing hijab.

The senior officers, who sat against the longer length of the table, leaned forward, and in their own little cliques, murmured amongst themselves. A senior female officer fixed Jack with a gaze that made him feel guilty even before sentencing.

'PC Appleyard, whilst this is not a criminal investigation, we do have the authority to take into account certain statements from interested parties.' She removed a single sheet of paper from a manilla folder. 'We have here a statement from Philip Parker, supported by his fiancée, Miss Amanda Ali.'

Jack had little choice but to acknowledge them, and the curtest of nods were exchanged. He held his breath.

'The statement has been made available to the members of the disciplinary panel. The statement made by Phil Parker exonerates PC Appleyard from any wrongdoing with regard to his actions on the night of the first of April 2022. He states that there was nothing that PC Appleyard could have done differently, given the circumstances. The statement further acknowledges that he may have been at fault for failing to ensure that the area was safe before entering the garden.'

Jack let out a silent breath. He could drive his trusty MINI Cooper a few more years yet. If that had been the financial cost to him for the truth being presented to the hearing, then it was a small price to pay. Any guilt that he felt about making the payment was tempered with the feeling of blame and self-recrimination he still felt almost daily in the months since that fateful night patrol.

'We will take a short half-hour recess, then present our verdict.'

Jack and his Police Federation representative retired to an allocated waiting room and fretted. Someone brought them a drink from a coffee machine which should have been decommissioned the previous decade.

Jack and the representative said little to each other. Circumstances had thrown them together for this short time, and they were unlikely to meet again after this day, regardless of the outcome.

As always, deliberations took longer than expected, and the coffee was almost cool enough to drink by the time they summoned him back twenty minutes later. Whilst they had made it clear at the outset that the panel was not a court of law, the general feeling took Jack back to the times when he had given evidence in magistrate and Crown Court.

'PC Jack Appleyard, please stand.' The chair of the panel had a prepared statement in front of her It looked very short, and Jack couldn't figure out whether this was a good or bad thing. Still relying heavily on his crutch, Jack stood and stared at the panel's chair.

'It was the original opinion of this panel that you were directly responsible for the injuries that were sustained by Special Constable Parker. You appeared to act in a reckless manner, which was likely to endanger life.'

Jack held on to one word in that statement: originally.

'Having received an impact statement from the injured party, however, we are minded to recognise that there were failings in the operational decision to deploy Special Constable Parker with you on that night. Additionally, he himself recognises that his behaviour, in particular the caution that should have been exercised when approaching the perpetrator of the crime, was not appropriate.' It was Amanda Ali's turn to appear concerned now. Any blame attributed to her fiancé could impact the compensation payments, far beyond the ten grand that Jack had paid her.

'Therefore, it is the decision of this panel that no further action will be taken against you with respect to this specific incident.'

Jack couldn't help but let out a whoop of relief. Inappropriate in the setting, but even his normally dour-faced Police Federation representative appeared surprised and relieved. The evidence against Jack had been substantial, if not overwhelming, and his representative had been warning Jack to expect the worst.

'However,' the panel's chair continued, 'subsequent events have come to the panel's attention which have a bearing upon your conduct as a police officer. These include an arrest on suspicion of impersonating a police officer and theft. This hearing has a duty of care to take into account PC Appleyard's professionalism. We cannot, in all good conscience, consider that you have acted at all times in a manner that represents the values that the West Midlands Police Force hold paramount.' The chair looked directly at Jack, her eyes locked with his. 'It is the final decision of this panel, therefore, that PC Appleyard is dismissed from the West Midlands Police from this date forward. All benefits accrued during his service will still be payable, but these will cease as from today. You may, if you wish, appeal against this decision.' She took off her glasses and put them down on the table, on top of her judgment. 'But I would urge you to consider very carefully if you would ever wish to work for an organisation which has quite frankly had enough of you.' Her final words were whispered and full of menace. The meaning was clear: don't mess with us and the decision we have taken, or you will regret it.

Days passed, and the stream of messages from former colleagues had slowed to a trickle. Jack had settled back into a routine of sorts, though compared to the excitement of a month ago, his days were mundane, to say the least.

The phone rang. In the days of WhatsApp and instant messaging, this was an unusual event for Jack, but even more so was the name that was displayed on the screen.

[Oscar Hot Drone Guy]

Jack paused the television programme he was watching and swiped right, accepting the call.

'Oscar?'

'Jack?'

'Er...' The silence seemed interminable, even though it probably only lasted a few seconds.

'How are you?' Oscar seemed almost as nervous as Jack, even though he'd initiated the call.

'I'm OK. Good, actually. You?'

'Yeah, I'm good, too. Saw your name on the BBC website.'

'Which headline? The "Double Murder Suspects Arrested" or "Reckless Copper Thrown Off Force for Endangering the Life of a Colleague"?'

'Both of them. I have to say, I preferred your photo in uniform'.

'Thanks, I think.'

'I... I don't suppose you fancy a drink sometime soon?' asked Oscar.

'I have some time on my hands. Tonight is good for me.'

'I'll pick you up at eight?'

'That's great. I've got someone I've got to meet this afternoon, but I'll be back from Brum in plenty of time.'

'Sounds intriguing,' Oscar said with a chuckle.

The phone call earlier in the week from Martin's father was another which came as a surprise to Jack. He guessed that Fifi had passed his name onto him, and who wouldn't be interested in meeting the man whose evidence had led to the arrest of both his son's killer and also his ex-wife?

Jack agreed to meet him in a neutral location, a coffee shop in Birmingham City Centre. The Cross-City line train deposited him at Birmingham New Street, and with the aid of Google Maps, he found the coffee shop on Church

Street. Jack remembered once he sat down, that he had been here before to meet a potential date here for a drink. It had not ended well, he seemed to recall.

He was worried about how he would recognise Benjamin Barr, but he needn't have worried. There was enough of a family resemblance between Martin and his father to make him instantly recognisable. Jack stood and they shook hands rather formally.

Benjamin looked every part the modern metrosexual, wearing tailored fit stone-washed jeans and a houndstooth jacket with leather patches over a skin-tight t-shirt that clung to abs that Jack would have been proud to own in his own mid-forties. Open University lecturer meets a young Rupert Everett, thought Jack.

'Thank you for agreeing to meet me.' Benjamin was softly spoken, without any trace of a Black Country accent. He seemed to have tried hard to create a new persona, Jack felt. He could hardly blame the man.

'Where do you live nowadays?'

'London, near Vauxhall. My partner and I have been there nearly fifteen years.'

'I was so sorry when I heard about Martin,' Jack continued. 'Though I never met him, we had chatted online. I've met some of his friends, though, including Fifi and of course poor Billy.'

'I hadn't seen my son for years. Not through want of trying, but Julie was dead set against any contact. She was obsessed about what would happen if Martin was gay.'

Jack rubbed his thigh at the point where the kitchen knife had severed his femoral artery. The walking stick was now just an affectation, but some days the pain was still there, deep in the tissue. 'I know that all too well. So, when did you last see him?'

'He was fourteen or fifteen, had just come back from a field trip somewhere in Wales. He was obsessed with the place, wanted us to go camping there in the summer holidays.'

'But you didn't go?'

'No. He mentioned to me at the time that he thought he preferred boys to girls. I told him to wait a few years and see how he felt then. He may change his mind. I know I wish I had waited a few years, for sure!'

'Did Julie know he'd spoken to you about this?'

'I'm guessing not,' Benjamin reflected, 'but Martin was always his mother's son. They probably had very few secrets at that time. I didn't mind the closeness they had, and I presumed at the time that Nick was a good stepdad to Martin. He could offer a better role model than me I thought.'

Jack stared at Benjamin. 'You don't need to be straight to be a role model.'

'Maybe. I still loved him, even though I never saw him. I made sure I paid my dues, too.'

'It seems most of that went on Nick's gambling debts, I'm afraid.' A pause. 'I think the house will have to be sold. You will be able to keep some of Martin's things, I guess.'

'Nick and Julie can sort that out. I have a few souvenirs from when he was at school, and that field trip report from Wales. How are Billy's parents taking it?'

'Rough, very rough. They want to make sure Julie is charged with hate crime as well as murder. The sentence won't be longer, but she'll have a tougher time in prison, maybe. It will take a year before it gets to court, and that's a long time to be in remand.'

'Were he and Martin seeing each other?' Benjamin asked. There seemed to be hope his voice.

'I suspect they might have been in the future. I think they "had fun",' Jack air quotes with his fingers, 'from time to time, but they were both too young to settle down.'

'You're probably right. I was too young to marry. My therapist agrees with me on that, anyhow.'

'What are you going to do now?' Jack asked.

'I've got a couple of friends still in the Midlands. I'll stop a day or so then head back home. Sirius will be missing me.'

'Your partner?'

'Our cat.' Benjamin smiled. 'Thank you for what you did. I'm sure Martin would have appreciated it too, and of course Billy's family.'

As they departed, Benjamin and Jack embraced as if they were old friends rather than acquaintances who had only just met.

The Mizan Spice restaurant was not particularly busy, but even so, the service was unusually slow, but this seemed to suit both Jack and Oscar; they had a lot to catch up on.

'Can we agree that we were both idiots that morning - me for snapping at you, and you for walking out like a spoiled kid?'

'A kid who needed spanking, maybe?' Oscar joked. Jack had missed that twinkle in his eye and lodged the information for possible future reference.

'I was just so caught up in trying to find out what had happened that day.'

'I can understand that, but we hardly knew each other. You spoke to me like I was one of your civvies in the station.'

'I've said I'm sorry, and I've also said that I'm grateful for you giving me a second chance.'

'Who said I'm giving you a second chance?'

'It was you who rang me, remember?'

'I may just have forgotten something at yours, like a pair of pants or...'

Jack could tell he was being teased and decided to go with it. 'No, no, I distinctly remember you putting your pants on, and being very disappointed at the time.'

'Well, that's a lie, because I was going commando. I had a good feeling about you even before we met.'

'And tonight... are you going commando again?'

'You may find out later.' Again that tease, and the little churn of Jack's stomach that came with it. He could feel himself blushing.

They ate their nargis kebab starters and ordered another beer each. Jack had caught a bus to the restaurant, intending to either taxi or catch a late bus back. He hadn't yet asked how Oscar had arrived, or indeed was getting home.

'A friend dropped me off.'

'A friend?'

'Yes.' Oscar replied, a little defensively. 'A friend. My housemate, actually. She was off to her yoga class, I bummed a lift.'

'So, how are you planning on getting back?'

'Depends where I'm going back to.'

Jack decided to ignore his flirty response, for the time being.

'What are you going to do with your time now?' Oscar asked, tracing his finger through the condensation on the side of his lager glass.

'Ah, glad you asked that,' Jack replied. This was the first time he'd had the chance to share with someone what he'd been planning for the last couple of weeks, to see what it sounded like when said out loud. He was surprisingly nervous and took another large gulp of beer. 'As you might have guessed, my career in the police is over.' He slapped his thigh. Whilst he had recovered well, Jack still walked with a slight limp, and was still a few months off being able to run again. The pounds had started to creep on, he had noticed. He would have to do something about that.

'Will you get compensation?' Oscar asked.

'I would have if I'd been on duty at the time. But I was just a civilian. There's a chance that I can claim something from the Criminal Injuries Compensation Authority, but that can take a while, and it will hardly be enough to retire on.'

'So what you going to do if you can't lead a life of decadent leisure?'

'Become a dick.'

'A what?'

'A dick - a private detective.'

'Really! I didn't think anyone actually did that in real life.'

'It's a bit niche I'll grant you, and you're the first person I've told. But it feels right for me, you know? I think there could be enough demand, and it will at least be a little more interesting than sitting on the sofa all day watching Homes Under the Hammer.'

'Don't you need all sorts of surveillance stuff - cameras and what not?'

'I can get that. What I can't get is expertise. I need someone who knows how to use the tech, set it up for me. Someone who knows... I don't know, about drones and that sort of thing.' Jack's pointed look was only spoiled by the waiter bustling around and delivering their main courses.

'Of course,' Jack continued, after carrying out an inventory of the various dishes, 'I'd be unable to offer much, if anything at the start. But there could be other benefits.' It was Jack's turn to smile, and for Oscar to flush.

'Do I get payment in advance?'

'Shall I order an Uber back to yours?'

Jack suppressed a slight shudder as Oscar mentioned Uber but forced a smile. 'Let's finish the meal first.'

EPILOGUE

The next time Jack met Benjamin was a crisp November morning. The first frost of Winter had nipped the grass and was taking time to clear in the weak Winter sun. Chasewater was an entirely different place, the summer days a long-distant memory. The wake-boarding centre had long shut up shop, and the only craft out on the water were some hardy windsurfers in full-body wetsuits.

The external conditions were lost on Jack, Oscar, Tracey, Gavin, and Benjamin who had travelled up specifically for the exhibition launch. In the main foyer of the Innovation Centre, some thirty images were hung. The photographer: Martin Barr.

The idea behind the exhibition came from Fish's parents, though they had found the idea of being at the launch themselves too upsetting and had sent their apologies. Jack and Oscar had done the lion's share of the work and had funded the printing. There was a donation box at the exit of the exhibition, with all money going to the Birmingham LGBT Centre.

Jack still fretted about the positioning of the photos, as warming mulled wine was being distributed amongst the attendees.

The exhibition ran in two parallel lines. Alongside one wall were Martin's pictures of the powerboat race, retrieved from the memory card of the cameras and equipment that had been found in Nick's locker. Technically, they were exhibits C and D in the upcoming trials. Tracey had however become a little more flexible in her own interpretation of the guidelines and had sneaked into the evidence store and copied the images onto her own laptop late one evening.

Jack knew nothing about photography and less about powerboats, but he was amazed at the quality of the images. The water under the hulls seemed almost alive, and even though nothing of the pilot's faces could be seen, their determination to win was perceptible through their grips on the rudder controls. He was not alone in his judgment of the photos; everyone seemed to be admiring the images.

The opposite wall was maybe less well received by the middle class, Middle England audience. There was no specific hostility, everyone was far too polite for that, but there was a sense that in this context the monochrome pictures of Fish were not appropriate. The images had been chosen carefully, and there had been no subterfuge needed to obtain the images - the high-resolution images were sat on Fish's laptop. The only manipulations that had Oscar had made to the images was switching them to monochrome, and adjustment of contrast to make them more artistically pleasing.

The images were in chronological order, starting with Fish smiling and staring at the camera, through the unbuttoning and removing his shirt, and the unzipping of his shorts, casually dropped on the floor. Only Jack and Oscar were aware that the striptease had continued further, much further, but even a lad in his underwear was causing some consternation.

The final picture was what was causing much of the consternation. Jack, Oscar, and his parents had agreed it was the most that they wanted to be revealed of Fish whilst it could still be considered 'artistic'. Everyone wanted it included however in an exhibition which was supposed to be as much a memorial to Fish as a tribute to Martin. Fish stood with a thumb placed either side of the waistband of his Calvin Klein trunks, pulling the underwear out slightly from his lean body. The faintest fuzz of hair was visible at the start of a trail from his flat stomach downwards. In the middle of Chasewater, in the midst of the heat of summer, he grinned back at Martin's camera without a care in the world.

Benjamin came over to look at the picture with Jack.

'I was never that confident at that age, were you?'

'No. I doubt I would be even now.'

Oscar rubbed a hand down Jack's thigh. 'I've told you, I think the scar is sexy.'

Jack smiled in return. 'I'm glad we arranged this.'

'Let's hope that the donations make a difference, too.'

They re-joined their friends, including a worried Tracey who thought that her fiancé Phil was maybe taking too much interest in the pictures of Fish. The crowds had started to thin. The exhibition was open for the full week, but Oscar and Jack knew that this wasn't the best time of the year for this sort of thing.

'Where do you fancy going afterwards?' Tracey asked the group.

'Dunno. It's too early to hit the pub, but I don't feel like just heading home.'

'We could always head to...' Jack was hesitant to complete the sentence.

'You were about to say the bloody BJ Diner, weren't you?' Gavin replied.

Benjamin looked confused. 'BJ Diner?'

'It's better than it sounds. Honest.'

The advert was posted online on all the usual sites, Gumtree, Shpock, Facebook Marketplace. Jack didn't know anyone who actually bought local newspapers nowadays, let alone read the classified ads.

'Private Investigation work for personal or

business. No job too small. Drone surveillance a speciality. Fully police checked. Contact Jack Appleyard on 07791 900 700.'

ABOUT THE AUTHOR

Andy Hollyhead

Andy Hollyhead is a semi-retired academic, who has lived in and around Chasewater for many years, and can be found walking its perimeter most days.

Andy has been writing for many years, and am part of Writing West Midlands Room 204 cohort, which develops writing talent in the area.

Whilst self-published, they are professionally edited. Please report any content error to me, so that this can be corrected for any future versions.

CHASEWATER MYSTERIES

Dead In The Water

The life of Martin Barr was narrow in scope, despite the vast expanse of Chasewater reservoir on his doorstep. The three major elements of his life, the supermarket he worked at, the small house he lived in with his mother and stepfather, and Chasewater, his favourite place to go were all within 500 yards of each other.

His tragic death came with more questions than answers. What was the motivation for killing him? And how did Jack Appleyard, suspended Police Constable with a history of his own know so much about how this happened, despite unable to access the official enquiry?

With the help (and hindrance) of friends, and strangers who become friends (and more), Jack stays one step ahead of the police, but at what cost?

Dead In The Closet

Jack Appleyard's Private Investigation business has yet to get off the ground, and he needs a job, if only to keep him busy through the long winter months. All is going well working at the local mining museum, and he seems to have a new circle of friends who seem to accept him and his new boyfriend Oscar.

But when a body is found in a store cupboard after one of Jack's shifts, and links are established not only to Jack's past, but also to other people in the museum, are new friendships and old relationships strong enough to be maintained?

Dead On Your Feet